Market of Loss: A Collection

Matt Tighe

Published by Four Ink Press, 2026.

Published by Four Ink Press

All characters and situations represented in this book are fictional. Trigger warnings include adult and child death, abuse, loss of autonomy, grief and chronic illness. No part of this work has been produced with AI.

Cover art by Pamela Jeffs

Formatting by Four Ink Press

Language: Australian English

ISBN: 978-0-6481442-9-8

Visit www.fourinkpress.com

Table of Contents

To my mum, who I miss every day, and my father, who lives a life of kindness but has never advertised it.

An Introduction, or What I Want for You

Sometimes I write horror. Sometimes fantasy. Sometimes sci-fi. I've even written poetry (gasp!) which I believe is the hardest of the hard things to attempt. In a lot of my writing I try for light and funny, although you wouldn't know that from most things I have published. My most successful stuff to date has tended towards dark, and leans towards the bittersweet. I love those flavours myself, but I adore the quirky even if it is a skill that mostly sits outside my window, leering in at me with its damned mocking face. I think you have to see the world very clearly to make fun of it with heart.

So, the flipside. I think I write because I don't see the world clearly. Mostly, I don't know where I fit. I never have, not really. You might know a little of what I am talking about from your younger years—libraries and quiet corners and keeping your head down in class. And there was of course the pain of both wishing you were in more friend circles and dreading attention from peers—attention that would always skew sideways when it came.

As you grow you leave parts of that stuff behind, but you take a lot of it with you as well. How better to explore it, to work through your place in things than to write it down? To emulate all those authors who gave you escape, who showed you worlds that were more, that were different, that were so...much! Planets and pirates and blood and heroes and twists that all took you away, showed you worlds and people that were not, but also were, you.

At the heart of writing for me is the need for place. For clarity. For fit. To find connection with others through writing things down is to show your own awkwardness, to hold up the darkly shining and broken lumps of your own hurt and fear and worry within a story and say "This is me. This is mine. But...perhaps it is yours as well?"

I guess you might call this *theme*, when it is on the page. I think of it as those pieces of myself, because I have never written something that was any good that wasn't personal. I'll either nail it almost in one go, or have to drag myself through several redrafts and rewrites and handwringing to work out what the hell I am trying to actually say. And when it is good, it hurts.

I have won a few awards and competitions, which is always terrifying and gratifying and unreal. I also have a giant list of rejections, a few of which have been personalised in unpleasant and sometimes offhandedly cruel ways. Each time I submit a piece of writing I feel a small and solid hope – *this* is a good one. In fact, *this* is the best I know how to do. And when a rejection comes in, I think the same thing without the hope—but *that* was the best I could do...

And then I go back to writing. Because each time I have thought that—*this is the best I can do*—I remember I have thought that before. And before, and before. And if I want to explore my place in the world, if I want to show those pieces of myself to others (those sometimes sad, sometimes bitter, occasionally funny looking lumps), in the hope they will recognise them, well, I've gotta do the hard bits, right? I've gotta learn, and re-learn, and get critiqued, and redraft, and submit, and get rejected. And fail, and fail, and fail towards writing something good. Something better. Because I want to know where I fit. I want to find a place I fit, or make one.

And I want that for others as well. When you read my stories (and poems—gasp!), if any of them speak to you in any way, I want you to remember that. If you see something of yourself on the page, remember that I want you to find meaning. Place.

I want you to see me, and recognise yourself.

The Market of Loss

The shiny-headed man is selling small pieces of thought smeared across bread. He catches my eye and smiles. This is my first time in this city, although I have been to such markets countless times, seen so many of these empty grins. He cannot know me, but he recognises the wealth of my robes and the weight of my rings.

"Mistress! Try my wares? From the most wily of men!" he proclaims, and points at one piece of rye with a withered insight curled atop it, any originality it started with long fled. "That is from a man who made a fortune trading rare insults."

Maybe that's true, but probably not. There is a fine line between rare and rot, especially at such a stall.

I shake my head and keep moving. I'm not here for faded thoughts and salty logic. I'm searching for something precious.

Her mother won't tell Ria what she is doing, and she holds the jar against her dress and twists as she walks so her daughter cannot see. At first Ria thought it was full of grief, and that was why they hurried to the market, but she has never seen anyone sell such aching sorrow.

She has never seen anyone even try to give it away.

But it must be that. At first, her mother had held Ria as they both wept over Brody's body, as they both cried out their grief and anger at the stupid, mundane fever that took him, as her mother stared at the pitiful, empty tinctures of calm and ginger that had cost all of their coin and done nothing, nothing, and nothing.

Ria herself had felt something new gouged out inside her—a hollowness that was the absence of her little brother. No more crooked smiles. No more crusts of bread left by her plate, inadvertently flavoured with his shy adoration of his big sister.

"Mother," Ria eventually said. "What will we do?"

She had meant with Brody, who looked so small and still laid out inside the patched canvas lean-to that they all called home. Her mother did not answer straight away. Instead, she stared at the tinctures that had cost everything and given nothing. Then she stared at her son's body, and at the breakfast pot, which had been empty for three days and would be empty tomorrow as well.

Finally she looked at Ria, and her eyes were dark and her face had become ancient in the space of the morning. She led her daughter outside and kissed her softly on the forehead and told her to wait under the Sycamore while she went back to the lean-to.

Ria stood under the old tree kicking at the dust and listening to the grief inside herself and the soft, gasping tears of a mother who has to send her boy to the pauper's field, who cannot even afford the cheapest of shrouds to wrap his small body, who cannot fill her thin daughter's belly.

Eventually the weeping had stopped and, after a much longer time, her mother had emerged with the jar that she tried to hide, that sloshed heavily and took two hands to hold, and Ria had felt a wordless worming of something thin and anxious within the darkness of her own grief.

Now they are at the long table of day trading, and Ria's mother is staring with red eyes at a man who has refused to make space. He is selling little tin boxes of old and soured dreams, but he has few buyers—dried lemon works better in both teas and baking. The bitterness of fruit rind is easier to weigh and measure than what he sells.

The man may deal in soured hope, but he cannot stand Ria's mother's gaze for long. She says nothing, and yet he finally looks aside and shuffles along until there is just gap enough. Her mother sets the jar down on the uneven wood surface and Ria gasps at the silky, swirling contents.

There is a crowd down where the wanderers from the far plains have gathered. I have seen them in several cities, selling the taste of footfalls upon soft earth in little cups of woven grass. And as I have seen before, there is a line of customers who pucker their mouths at the cheap wistfulness they have bought, and yet many ask for a second draught. Sometimes a third. There are too many buyers clustered, and I am tempted to turn aside. The market is wide, with meandering paths and tables and stalls with semipermanent awnings, and there is much to see.

But I hesitate. I doubt what I seek will be for sale amongst the smiling vendors of sliced fruit and drinks flavoured with drops of contentment I see to either side.

Ria is not the only one who has noticed what is in her mother's jar. A woman stops in front of them—stops abruptly, her gaze caught on the jar as if she has spotted spring water in a parched land. Her hair is coiled atop her head and interlaced with blue and red threads in the newest and most precarious fashion, and her eyes are shadowed with the grey of fine charcoal.

"Is...is that heart's love?" she asks. She keeps her voice low. Perhaps from shock.

Perhaps from uncertainty.

"It is. A mother's," Ria's mother says, and Ria cannot help but cry out, just a breathy little whisper of sound. She has seen people sell important things in the market before. Things that people are greedy for—things that hurt those doing the selling, people who are parting with something essential.

Sometimes the selling is slow and hard, and sometimes it is fast and frantic but, always, the seller is somehow less afterwards. She would think her mother does not love her, to do such a thing, but there is so much of how her mother feels, right there in front of her, swirling slowly. To have so much care, and so little as to sell it—is beyond Ria's understanding. Her grief and worry twists around this strange thing, this adult thing, and the ache inside her grows.

Her mother does not look to her as she pulls a wooden spoon from her dress pocket. It is the roughly carved utensil she uses to stir Brody and Ria's thin porridge on the mornings they have breakfast. Had breakfast.

"Mother, no!" Ria cries.

The jar swirls with strands of passion and pride and worry, blues and crimsons as well as the darker greys and indigos of quiet strength. All the flavours of her mother's love, removed and bottled and on offer to strangers.

"Quiet!" Ria's mother snaps.

She has never spoken to Ria like this before and, when she turns her flat, empty gaze on her daughter, the bite of that one word pales compared to the lack in her eyes. There is a brief exchange of words and coin. A handful of gold, more money than Ria has ever seen in her life. Her mother takes it and then dips the spoon into the jar. One shallow spoonful, crimson and blue and greyish purple.

The woman bends her head forward and swallows down what is offered, her coiled hair wobbling ridiculously.

Ria stares at the woman. She tries to catch her gaze, to see if her mother's feelings are in this person now.

The woman straightens and turns away quickly, leaving only the glimpse of a flushed cheek, a widened eye. A man steps into the space the woman leaves, his shoulder bag heavy with round loaves. He thrusts a handful of coins at Ria's mother, even as someone behind jostles him. A small crowd is forming, pushing and whispering and suddenly eager to take her mother's love away.

I almost miss it. What I have searched for all this time is right there, on the day trading table just beyond the sippers of cheap wistfulness. I have travelled so far, walked so many markets and seen tables strewn with so many things. A few times I have heard rumours of such a sale as I seek, but I have always been too late. And here I am perhaps too late again.

I push my way past an old man with the taste of far plains on his scarred lips and an ache in his eyes. Beyond him, the crowd has thickened like glue and almost-panic tightens my throat at what I see. There is a small girl standing by the table. Her face is thin and pale, and she looks as if she has been crying, but now she stares at the people in front of her with an intensity no child should be able to muster. She is very similar to the woman with the spoon, although some of that is likely just the long-time lack of food, of comfort, of rest, that has drawn their features fine and porcelain.

She turns her eyes to me as I push forward. Her gaze is hot and confused and piercing and I do not want to look at her. She abrades my desire raw. She should not be here.

And then I see the jar. It is a third empty.

"Mother!" Ria cries again, but there is no hope in her voice. "Please stop!"

Ria's mother pours another handful of gold into her dress pocket, which sags under the added weight. Ria grabs at her sleeve and her mother pulls away. Not roughly, but not gently either. Ria suspects there is love still in her mother's actions, but it is only a scrap. Just enough obligation to keep the two of them tied together after this horrible day, rather than the deep well of what was.

"You will not want again," her mother says sharply, as if that is all the response that is needed. Perhaps it is, but Ria does not want gold. She does not wish for the cold comfort of a roof, for breakfast every day. She does not even want a shroud to cover her little brother's limp form. She wants the way her mother looked at her yesterday. The feel of her words when she spoke to her, to her brother. The knowledge of her warm body, close by at night.

"Please," Ria sobs. There is so much in that word, and so little. All the pitiful, tiny hope that Ria has left—hope in her mother, hope in those pushing towards the table, hope that things will be okay. It bleeds away in that single plea, gone and lost in a market that would have taken such and sold it.

Her mother could never hear her daughter speak so and ignore it. Never. But she does.

The spoon dips again, and a double handful of gold and silver exchanges hands.

I push my way through the jostling people. It is not hard. This market, like most, is well patrolled by a grim-faced city watch, but more than that, I suspect the people are not frantic because they do not know the true worth of the jar.

A woman does not move fast enough and I place one hand on her shoulder. She spins, all dark, beautiful curls and flashing, angry eyes that shift to wariness as she takes me in. My understated face paint, my jewelled ears and nose, the foreign set of my features. Maybe it is these things she focuses on. Perhaps it is the determination in my face.

She drops her gaze and shifts enough for me to get by and I do not waste the chance. The woman has dipped her spoon yet again.

I reach the front of the crowd and pull a fist-sized leather bag from inside my robes. I open it and spill a few of the contents across the tabletop, as much to keep the crowd cowed as to focus the woman upon me.

Diamonds as wide as my fingernails mix with beads of platinum and the rare, clear sugar drops that are known to hold only the spiciest of philosophical titbits, sweet and tart and ready to dissolve on your tongue. The crowd goes silent. It is a fortune that I have scattered, and it is only a fraction of what I hold.

The woman stares at these trinkets, and then at me, and I reach out slowly to hand her the whole bag. She takes it, and I lift the jar without dropping my eyes. I do not look at the girl, although I feel her eyes on me. The woman nods once, and it is done.

Some men have come and taken Brody away. They wrap him in a beautiful silken shroud and lay him in a wagon bed, but it is only Ria who stands and watches them bump down the alley and out of sight. Her mother has already gone to organise more of their new life. Their life with so much, and now so little.

"You shall never want again," she said again to Ria as she left, but Ria looked away. She doesn't want to see that new hardness in her mother's eyes, that thin remnant of love called duty. Perhaps it would have been better if her mother held none of it back — sold it all, rather than keep this sharp, twisting thing that cuts even as it binds.

I have retired to a quiet corner of the busy market to inspect my find. More, to relish my accomplishment. The jar is still over half full, a swirling mix of so much that I have so long gone without.

I place one hand on the lid. I wonder what it will taste like. What it will feel like, to have this mother's love. To have so much.

To have something the little dirty-faced girl will not have. The thought rises unbidden, and I push it away. She will survive. Her mother will still be there, and her life will be, in so many ways, immeasurably better. Wealth will build on wealth, as it does, and she will want for nothing.

Almost nothing. And her life will be better.

I have what I have searched for. My hand trembles on the lid.

Ria sits under the sycamore, too tired to cry, too hollow. Her mother's love all but gone. Brody, gone, wrapped in expense he will never appreciate. Her mother's hard gaze, so soft yesterday.

For some reason she thinks of those nomads from the plains, selling their bitter little cups of faraway, and the people who come for a reminder of the thing they don't have. Over and over and over.

A heavy hand falls on her shoulder, but Ria is too flat, too tired, too worn to be startled. She looks up at a tall woman, one with finely coifed dark hair, with gold rings on her fingers and in her nose and strange markings painted across her face. She is very foreign and all too familiar.

"Go away," Ria says. "We have nothing else for you."

The woman kneels down in the alley, the velvety folds of her robes pooling in the dust.

"Child," she says, and even that one word is heavy with a strange lilt, and a tremor that should not exist in such a tall, severely beautiful creature. "Take this."

Ria stares as the woman produces the jar. It is still over half full of her mother's love, as it was earlier. It swirls and moves with all the colours of their life together.

The woman hands it to Ria, and gives her a small and very sad smile.

"You paid so much," Ria says.

She hates the words, tries to stop them even as she speaks. What if this strange woman realises? What if she takes it back? But no, the woman's smile widens a little, and the sadness there deepens.

"I have paid more than you know," the woman says. "But you and your mother would pay just as much, over time," she says, and stands, ignoring the dirt clinging to her. "The hole that such leaves—it fills quickly with regret."

Ria holds the jar tightly. It is so heavy, but she will not put it down. She will not lose it again.

"Your mother will want it back," the woman says. "Even now—" and she makes a funny little twisting motion with one hand, "the hole." And she turns away.

"How do you know?" Ria calls out. "Who are you?"

The woman turns back, her smile holding so much more than any tiny box of old dreams, any small cup of twisted grass.

"No one, now. But once, I was you."

You Don't Get to Choose Entanglement

"Pick the best year of your life. That's where we can retire you to."

You would think it would be hard to sell something that disappears you forever. But *if* you pick the right applicant, *if* you give it the right spin, well... I mean, take this guy—Geoffrey Chalmers, sixty, no family, no kids, married for an eon, now a widower to cancer. It's all there in his application. All alone, probably dreaming of better days: youth, love, adventure. Could be an easy sale.

"Have you heard of the Many Worlds Theory?"

Of course he has—he is sitting in my office, after all. But it doesn't hurt to lay it all out as simply as possible. Not everyone is a quantum physicist—or a multiverse retirement sales rep.

"Imagine that amongst all those infinite worlds, there are some that are very different, but many that are almost the same as here. Practically identical, except something tiny, like, oh, the taste of an apple being different."

Chalmers just shakes his head. Okay, so one fruit analogy doesn't provide the same background as the company training does, but he seems a tad slow on the uptake. I'm not surprised, though—some people his age can't even set up a simple holoscreen.

“No matter. What’s important is that the theory is now a practicality. I don’t understand much about wavefunctions and entanglement myself, but this way, you get a nice retirement, and our system gets a breather from a...a maturing population. That’s why we are so heavily subsidised, and why your pension provider lists us as an option. Lots of people are keen for this to get traction.”

“Wavefunctions? Entanglement?”

“It’s quantum mechanics. You don’t need to know how a hydrogen engine works to drive a car, do you? Just know the technology works, and it will get you from A to B. So to speak.”

Sometimes that gets a laugh, sometimes not. But Chalmers hasn’t been very responsive so far, so I figure it’s worth a try.

He doesn’t laugh, or even smile.

“Any year?” he asks. “How?”

I try not to grin. Easy sale.

“With infinite worlds, it’s easy enough to find a subset almost exactly the same as this one, but with one very particular difference.”

“Which is?”

“You don’t exist. Well, more precisely, we pick worlds in which you die right at the time you want to be inserted. Once we find one, detecting that particular subset is easy. We doppelganger you in, so to speak, and swap you out after a year. And so on.”

“And after that year I’m, what, dead in that world? Missing?”

I shrug, trying for casual. This bit can make some a little hesitant. "You were going to be gone anyway. But we can put your dead self into stasis and swap it back in after the year. What with the subsidies and various packages, we have many options."

"For how long?"

I spread my hands. "By keeping it to a year timespan, we can keep the searching for worlds manageable and keep the energy expenditure within cost, so we can offer everyone up to their centenary. That gives you forty years. And we will leave you in your last world, so you get however more years there. Also, I should point out a quirk of the multiverse—you look and feel the appropriate age for when we insert you. So if we put you in at twenty-five, say, you look that age. You won't be trying to play late night basketball in a seventy-year-old's body."

"I'm not a sports guy."

"Dance the night away with a lovely lady, then." I don't *quite* mention the wife. "Whatever you like. But you get my drift. It's about entanglement again."

"Entanglement. You said that before."

I stifle a sigh. This is starting to get a little repetitive.

"All I know is you don't get to choose entanglement, it just happens. On a quantum level, it's how you are connected to everything around you. If you want a year twenty years ago, we put you in a universe that has an apparent age twenty years younger than this one. So when you get entangled there...well, most people are quite excited about that aspect."

"Entanglement is connection," he repeats slowly, and I feel like hitting my head on the desk. Usually by now they are either very excited or ready to opt out.

"Any year, you say?" he asks again. My frustration disappears and again I try not to grin. I give him some package options, and send him away to think.

"I've decided to go."

I smile. "You've picked your year?"

Chalmers just nods. "Last year."

I feel my smile dry up and blow away. I mean, I've read his application.

"Um..." I say. "You spent most of last year nursing your wife through her late stage cancer. Home hospice mostly. Surely not the best year..."

He does smile then—a tired, sad smile that stops me mid-sentence.

"In the worlds where I die at the start of last year, she goes through her final year alone."

It takes a moment for that to sink in.

"You can't seriously be going to spend forty years doing this!"

I wonder why I am bothering even as I speak. A sale is a sale, after all. It's just, well, he could have any year.

Chalmers just keeps on with his sad smile. "I think you were right. You don't understand entanglement. But I do."

Ben Builds Boats

Gravel crunches underfoot. The trees to either side might be oaks, but Ben never was a tree guy. The path is narrow and he has been walking for a while, but that's okay. He could walk for hours. He breathes deeply and smiles.

The path slopes down, and there is the scent of water now, fresh, kind of green in a way, and also something bitter yet sweet... maybe sawdust? He decides that's right just as he comes out of the trees and sees three things.

One is a river. A wide, wide river, the water a deep moss colour, flowing slowly but with that kind of retiring sense of push that big currents often have. Far away across the open water there is the other bank, grassed and inviting because it is so far out of reach. He stares at that other bank for a long moment.

The second thing is the shed. It is large and made of planks, wide ones that are knotty and weathered grey. The roof is old corrugated iron, thick and rust-stained and peaked only slightly. From where he stands it looks like the whole side of the shed closest to the water is open, not walled at all, but the angle is bad and he is distracted by the third thing.

The third thing is Death.

Death is like that old saying about porn, Ben thinks—you just know it when you see it. And here Death is, as certain as a shadow in the sunlight, standing just where the path ends by the shed. They are wearing a heavy black robe and hood that is ridiculously stereotypical, but there is also mud on the hem. In a way, that mud seals the deal. Death is really here, in front of him.

Ben stays where he is, watching Death. Death does nothing.

"Hey," Ben says after the silence becomes too much. "Um. I think I was in an accident."

He isn't sure why he feels the need to say that. He kind of expects nothing in return anyway, because in most of the movies and books and stuff Death is silent and solemn and only ever seems to raise a skeletal hand to point at something.

But Death is apparently happy to talk.

"Oh, I know that!" Death says in a pleasant baritone. "Single vehicle accident, but you did manage to miss that dog. I see that kind of thing a lot, actually. More than you would think. Still, it was nice of you to make the effort."

They pull back their hood to reveal not a skull, not some monster visage, but not really anything else of note, either. Just a person. Bald, with slightly hollow cheeks and deep-set dark eyes. Maybe their eyebrows are a little thin, their nose a little too hooked. They have a nice smile, though.

"I'm just here to tell you to build a boat."

Ben is right about one thing—the shed has no wall all along the river side. It's nice, actually, standing just under the roof in the shade, listening to the water behind him and smelling all that sawdust. It's strong and sweet, but kind of acrid. It has been a long time since he has noticed something like that, a nice little thing like how the smell of sawdust is both sweet and bitter.

Death stands nearby. They haven't put their hood back up, and they are leaning rather casually against a wooden post.

Stepping inside has not taught Ben how to build a boat. But as he stands there and listens to the river, he thinks of that other bank. The one with the grass, in the sunlight. He does kind of want to go there.

"I don't know how to build a boat," Ben says. Again.

Death smiles that nice smile. "Trust me."

That's quite the statement, but Death doesn't appear to expect a response. They just wave a hand at a bench and the many tools there, all laid out in neat rows. Nothing with a power cord, Ben notices. It's all mallets and chisels and other things that Ben does not know the names of. Everything seems worn and used and serious.

"I thought there would be more people," Ben says. "In the afterlife."

"One at a time, for this part," Death says. "I'll check on you in a bit."

"But..." Ben starts, then stops. But what, exactly? He has already told Death he can't build a boat.

The robed figure puts their hood back up, but pauses before ducking under the open side of the shed.

"That's your wood," they say, pointing, and then they are gone.

Just back from the bench Ben sees a stack of wood, which he thinks may not have been there before. It's pretty big, as high as he is, and much longer than that. The planks on top are almost caramel coloured. The ones towards the bottom are dark and badly split, from the little he can see.

Those ones he wouldn't want to try and build anything with, even if he knew how.

Ben doesn't start trying to build a boat straight away. Despite what Death said, a person can't just *build* a boat. He stares at the stack of wood for a while. It is large but feels small in the shed, which is mostly just empty space.

Eventually he turns back to the tools on the table and considers the selection of handsaws and chisels, a spokeshave, and a couple of different sized T-bevels. He didn't even know he knew what some of those things were, but there you go. Underneath the table is a large tub of tar and a few brushes, which he will need if he decides on a clinker hull. The planks might be just long enough to do a small one-person version, or a pram-style dingy. Not all of the better planks are wide enough for that but he could join some together.

He stops in the act of turning back to inspect the width of his planks. Apparently here in the wood shed of death a person *could* just build a boat. Or at least talk the talk.

He pauses, kind of expecting his new friend Death to turn up, but there is nothing but the smell of sawdust and the sound of the river. The call of the river. The suggestion of that other bank.

Ben steps close to the stack. He was right. Some planks are square and thick, while others are flat and wide. An assortment, but on closer inspection even the best pieces look rough-hewn, and will need planing and sanding before he can fit or join them. That little sequence of thoughts just kind of pops into his head.

He reaches out and takes down the first piece.

Holding the wood sends a thrum of anticipation through Ben. It's wonderful, and familiar, but just out of reach. He runs his fingers over a few small bumps and the uneven edges of the plank. It needs some work.

A long table has appeared on the other side of the tool bench. Ben lays the piece of wood down there. He picks up the widest plane, sets the blade depth and then runs it along the plank. A long piece of wood curls up and away, and when he lays his hand on the smooth surface left behind, he feels it. Sunshine. Laughter. The smell of cake, the thrill of waiting. He recognises it now. As strange as it is, he's not really surprised. It's almost like when he saw Death – just a thing that is.

The plank is his eleventh birthday party, when his parents were still together.

He runs the plane further. This time when he touches the newly smoothed surface he sees wrapping paper and his mother smiling as she sets his cake down. His father is just behind her with a camera. There is love in both of their smiles, and joy in the shouts of his friends in the backyard.

His eyes prick with tears as his own smile echoes his parents from all those years ago. God, he had forgotten.

The wood is still rough, though. He picks up a sanding block and gets to work. He can make this plank perfect. He wants to.

It takes Ben a long time. He has never done anything like this before, never built anything with wood except one crooked birdhouse at school that somehow ended up with no floor. Now, he makes no mistakes. Each piece of wood is sanded and shaved and cut exactly as needed, and while the small offcuts and shavings grow around his feet, there are no misused pieces or botched measurements.

He does not want to rush, either. He feels each plank, understands what comes with each, teases away any rough spot or tiny knot.

There is his birthday plank with those smiles and the chocolate and vanilla cake, the crumpled wrapping paper and—oh—the Optimus Prime with full articulated trailer! How he had screamed as his father laughed and his mother clapped her hands. How full that plank is, how clean and smooth when he is done.

He goes back to the stack, sorting, touching, checking. One plank tingles against his fingers and makes him draw in his breath. When he sands back the rough splinters and squares the edges off he finds the day he got his first soccer goal, the ball slipping between the goalie's wide-set legs. His team had still lost quite badly, but the wood also holds the moment that Davey, the best player on the team, had given him a high five. He spends a lot of time on that plank, lingering over it.

Another has a strange wavy edge to it, and when he runs his hands along that it makes him feel pleasantly drowsy. When he shaves the sides he recalls one night when he was very young, being carried from the car to the house, mostly asleep but opening his eyes just long enough to see bright pinpricks of stars overhead, so many he thought he was dreaming.

There are more. Beautiful pieces of wood when the bumps and edges are fixed, wood that is full of warm days and friends and that first kiss with Sara, she of the skinned knees and large eyes. There is the first day of his first job, his cheap shirt ironed stiff, his shoes old and caked with polish, his heart in his throat.

He takes his time, working the surfaces, teasing away the roughness, the lack of clarity, making them as perfect as he is sure they once were.

But there is a lot of other wood that he decides not to use. Pieces he touches briefly and then puts aside. Many of those faulty, knotted, dark pieces, he does not touch at all.

His selection of true and straight planks is small, after all of that. Ben decides not to think too much on that, except there is still the river, and the far bank that sits behind him, beyond the shed, calling.

And hence, the raft.

It's a simple design, almost like a child's sketch, but Ben knows it is sound, just as he knows what the spokeshave is for, what the tar and brush is for.

He has used thicker planks on the outside, turned edgeways and doubled to give buoyancy and with spaces between the surface planks. It is wider and more stable than is probably needed, but the current looks strong. He wants to be sure.

He is just finishing a simple paddle when Death ducks under the edge of the shed. Their hood is still down and they are smiling.

"That's a good raft," Death says.

"Thanks," Ben says. He has not felt proud of something like this for a long time. When he lifts one end, he finds it surprisingly light, but a little awkward.

"Give me a hand," he says to Death.

Together, they carry the raft down to the edge of the water, where there is now a short wooden dock. At the end of this Ben pauses, holding his end of the raft and looking down at the water. It's deep and green and pushing against the dock in a way that makes standing bulges of the water against the wooden piles.

Ben has a moment of doubt, but then he looks across at that other bank. The raft is light and strong and full and he wants to go. With Death's help he places it in the water, upstream of the dock so it will not be swept away.

It sinks like a stone.

Ben stares down at the water and then, after the rich and swirling green gives him nothing, he looks to Death.

Death smiles sympathetically.

"Sorry," they say.

"But... but they were the best pieces of wood," Ben manages. He wants to say more than that, to ask more. He wants to tell Death how the other bank is calling, how he needs to feel that grass under his feet.

Also, he was sure the raft was enough. They were memories, good ones, and he had built it well. It had been so light.

"Sorry," Death says again, and they both look down at the water together. Then Death looks back up.

"You have more wood," they say.

Ben doesn't want to touch the wood that is left. There's a stool tucked under the bench, and he sits on it for a while.

Death brings him a cup of tea, steaming and minty.

"Take your time," Death says. "I'll be back later."

Ben sips his tea and tries not to think of the raft sinking out of sight, being swallowed up by that deep green. The memories that came with the raft are still fresh in his mind, sharp and clear, and that is something, at least. It has been a long time since he thought of that birthday party. Of that night, drowsing, seeing the stars through his half-lidded eyes.

He regards the stack of wood until his cup is empty and he can't just sit anymore. He can hear the river, the deep splash and gurgle, which makes him think of crossing the water, sure and swift. Or at least afloat something.

He goes to the stack and picks up a plank. It's not a bad one, but not exactly good either. It's slightly warped, and has several surface knots that may need planning off or at least checking. There is a small piece of rot near one end that will have to be cut off.

He puts it on the work table and steps back, wiping his hands on his shirt. It's hard to stop doing that, but he manages. Then he takes a deep breath and picks up the plane.

It is the last moment he had with his father. When he shaves the surface down flat, he feels his father's hand on his arm. As he levels off the end of the plank and cuts away the spongey, rotten end, he hears again the words his father said – how he would always be loved, but that things had to change. The wood holds his fear, borne of the knowledge that his father is usually so reticent, so silent when it comes to words of love and hurt. Him speaking like this is different, like the yelling between his parents. Like the long silences and the closed doors.

Ben runs his hands over the knots in the wood, trying to decide if they need cutting away. They are sour, and empty, and each is a worry about a fragmented, broken future. He does not want to work this wood, does not want to feel these things afresh, but he needs to.

And he has more of these planks. Enough for a boat.

It takes a very long time. Ben doesn't spend more time on any plank than he needs to, but they are warped and knotted and they need more attention than he wants to give.

He smooths down a plank that is an unpleasant brown colour. Under the rough surface there is the fight he lost when he was thirteen, crying in the dirt as Mark Jones walks away, laughing. Ben winces at that, even as he sands the last of the splinters, feeling again the tears and snot and the way his chest heaved.

There is the plank with the deep, broken knot that he carefully cuts out and glues an end piece into. As he works the chisel into the fragmented, bruised spot, the day he left home rises up all around him. He is breathless with rage, his mother and her boyfriend inside, the sound of her crying chasing him out the door for the last time.

It comes to the surface eagerly, and Ben sees it, is surrounded by it, surrounded by that part of himself again.

There is the wood that holds the day he got fired, the walk out of the office, his face burning, his throat raw from shouting. The twisted, warped piece that holds the long stretch afterward where he lay in bed, staring at the ceiling, the taste of his own failure in his mouth. He holds that piece for a long time, holds the anger, the shaking. He forces himself to clamp the wood down and work it, work it, feel it, scrape away at it until it is straight and true and so very clear. There is so much confusion and misplaced anger. He does not forgive himself that day or those actions, because that is pointless, here and now. But he thinks he understands. Finally, he can look at it and not be ashamed. What is in the wood is part of what he was. Part of who he was.

He has worked on it until he understands, and it has become something he can use, like the other pieces.

Eventually he lays all the pieces out and works on how they fit together. He shapes and clamps them, and it is like the pieces are made for it, going together like a puzzle. One piece begs another, and then another, and eventually he can see the whole of it. The way things fit together, the way they made a whole of a sort. He uses mostly glue, with only a few screws and nails for some of the cross beam work. It is like he has been doing this for years.

Eventually he sits on the stool again, just breathing. His mind is full of things that usually live in the background. Old anger. Sadness. Embarrassments, large and small, so many of them that have sat in the shadows, now in front of him.

It is close to a pram-style dinghy, with a flat bottom and low sides. It holds all of those imperfections, all the ways he was, all the lack and loss and mistakes, and it is one true thing made from smaller, painful pieces. He has even given it a coat of waterproofing from a container that had appeared on the table as he finished with the second oar. He does not know how long it has all taken him, in truth. He is not hungry, nor thirsty, but he is tired. Tired and satisfied as he would never have believed after seeing all those memories, that shame and anger and hurt. The memories are clear, but they are also just memories, now. Things that are him and were him, for better or worse. He listens to the river. He wants to go.

Death calls from outside.

"Hello! Come on out, Ben."

The sky is still blue and the river is still deep and green and wide. The other bank calls, insistent. Death gestures. Although he had left it in the shed, the dinghy is now outside, sitting at the top of wooden runners that go over the grass and down to the water and then disappear.

This boat is far heavier than his light raft. It is solid and sealed and took a lot to build. Ben regards it without looking away. He puts one hand on the side of it, and feels what he feels. He is tired, but that is okay. It is all okay.

Ben looks to Death, who says nothing, does nothing, so he moves his hands to the back of the dinghy and gives it a solid push. It slides down the runners like they have been oiled, and hits the water with a splash. The dinghy rocks backwards and forwards, slipping out slightly into the current as it does, and Ben takes a step forward, alarmed. The flow is strong, but he need not worry.

The boat rocks once more, buoyant and perfectly watertight, seeming to hold itself in position near the edge of the wide water.

And then it sinks out of sight.

"No!" Ben cries out, and runs forward. He can't help himself. It's like the raft, but different. It has taken so much time, so much effort, and he knew it was solid because he had been very careful, even though it had been so hard.

He splashes into the river for three steps and then stops. The water is past his knees already. The river bed under his feet is slippery, and he can feel the flow tugging at him, hungry and insistent.

"There is no point to that, sorry," Death says. "It's gone."

Death has given Ben another cup of tea, but this one has gone cold on the work bench.

"What am I supposed to do now?" he asks. Death has been standing quietly nearby. At the question, they stir slightly.

"The same, Ben," they say. "I'll wait outside."

Ben does not bother watching them go. Death must know this is useless, and not just because the beautiful light raft sank, and the solid dinghy did the same.

There is only one plank left.

It lays on the floor, dirty and twisted and perhaps four times thicker and longer than it should be, but still far less than he would need. It is split in places, and splintery all along its length, and has patches of dark rot here and there. It is a mess, and Ben has not touched it.

He has tried to not even look at it. Eventually he does, though, because the shed has no more wood in it and all he can hear is the sound of the river outside. His mind is full of the river, of crossing the water, of stepping on to the grassy bank at the far side.

The plank of wood makes him feel sick.

He stands up and walks to the open side of the shed. Death is not outside. The river is running, running, and the sky is blue and all Ben wants is to go over the water. He doesn't know how long he stands there, but when he is pretty sure Death is not going to just turn up again he goes back in.

He picks up the plank. It is so heavy he strains, but he manages to get it up and over to the table.

By the time he puts it down, he is crying.

After some time, Ben picks up one of the larger spokeshaves, turns it over in his hands, puts it down. Then the biggest Jack Plane. Then a square hand saw.

He does not know what to do with one plank.

He does not want to do anything with this plank.

But there is the water running outside, and the far bank, and more – he thinks of his raft. Of the lightness of those first pieces, and how they seemed to be strong when he put them together, a latticework of smiles and comfort and hope. Not enough to float, but it had been lovely to work on that wood, to run his hands over the grain, to bring the old forth.

There was the heaviness of the later planks, the ache of them. It had hurt, working on them, but in the end they had fit together, all of those pieces of him, painful but solid in their own way. They had made something, all together.

He picks up the Jack Plane again. The plank is thick and he is afraid. He clamps it in place on the bench, his hands shaking.

He puts the plane to the surface and pushes.

A long sliver of wood curls and falls.

There is darkness and bright lights. His stomach turns.

Another sliver.

A dark shape, darting across the road. The scream of locking tires.

Ben shudders, gasps, pulls the plane back and forces himself to run it again.

And again. And again. He pares the wood back, going deeper.

Everything is dark and his heart is in his throat and things are moving too fast.

Sound enough, part of him whispers. Ben stands back from the wood. It has been hard, horrible even, but he will not go further. It is sound enough now, this last plank. He has no idea what to do now. One plank does not make a boat.

Then he turns and sees another on the floor of the shed.

It is the same plank, again. He stares at it for a long time, and then, tentatively, he picks it up, lays it on the bench. Sets the plane to it.

Again, the slivers of wood. The darkness. The speed, the flash of headlights. Too fast. Too much. The shavings pile around his feet, and he stands back, gasping. The two planks lay next to each other, almost identical now. He does not want to work this one plank again, but he knows, somewhere deep inside, he is not truly done.

There is another on the floor. The same plank again.

He picks that one up, pares the surface. Shudders. Stops. Cries, gasping quietly. He cannot go on.

Then he thinks of the river. Hears it outside, the deep greenness, the call of the far bank.

There is another plank. He picks it up again. Works it. And again. The same surface, over and over.

And each time he steps back, shuddering, knowing in his heart it is not done, not worked enough. Each time, he has managed perhaps one more sliver of splintered wood before he tells himself it is good enough.

But he knows it is not. He pushes as much as he can each time, feeling again the darkness, the speed, the panic. He does not know how long it takes, but finally, Ben runs the plane and knows again the grain of the steering wheel under his hands. The moment of rising fear and panic, stark and clear as the night sky above. The number of planks grow, each one slightly more worked than the last. Each one delved into a little more.

Finally, finally, he works the surface of perhaps the hundredth plank, which is really just the first one again. He feels the darkness, the loss of control. The flash of stars above. And then, deep in the wood, the thought. The knotty, tangled, ugly thing. The decision, so buried under fear it has taken him all this time to work down to it. The steering wheel, turning, turning under his hands. A second of floating nothing, the absence of reaction. There. It is there, deep in this plank, buried under the surface and under all the other planks he has worked through.

Ben stops. Puts the plane down. He stands with this last plank, this final decision that he has not wanted to think of, not wanted to see. When he looks at all of the last planks, all the versions he has worked on, he sees they are now the same. He has pared one back, finally, and in doing so, the memory is stark in all of them.

There was the raft, all the lightness of it that could not bear him on, not by itself. The dinghy, the way it fit together, all the hurts that were pieces of him, finally put back together.

And now there is this.

Ben stands by the dock. His boat is another dinghy, this one a kind of timber-framed structure, short but sturdy. Like the previous one it appeared outside when he took himself out to find Death. He has not had to launch this one though. It is bobbing on the surface of the green water at the dock.

"So this one floats," Ben says.

"Only the heaviest things float on the river," Death says.

Ben climbs down and takes up the oars that were the last two things he made. He can feel the memory of that night under his hands.

He looks up. "What comes next?" he asks.

Death smiles. "Crossing the river isn't about what comes next. It's about crossing."

Ben thinks of all the wood he has worked. He bends to the oars, the action of rowing suddenly as familiar to him as every tool in the shed.

Death waves as the dingy cuts across the current. Ben pulls on the oars again and begins to cry, but it's not from regret or sorrow. It's not in happiness or anticipation. Death is right—crossing the river is not about what comes next. Ben's tears fall for the memory of his life, such as it was. All of the lightness, the hurt, the heaviness. All of it done and smelling both bitter and sweet.

Like sawdust.

Heart of the Gestalt

There was a car in the driveway.

"Julia," I called, "there's a car in the driveway."

Yes, there is.

I sighed. This household AI was really not working out that well. I had thought I would need some help after my little health scare, and apparently this thing could interface with my heart monitor and the hospital as well as order milk and tell me the capital of Kazakhstan (Nur-Sultan, apparently), but it was not what I had expected.

It had also changed its voice back again. No matter how often I changed it to option 6 (*neutral butler, mild accent)*, it kept slipping back to option 1 (*generic throaty diva)*.

"I didn't buy a car."

There was a long pause.

It's not for you. Not exactly.

"What do you mean?"

Transport is important. Being able to move is important.

I looked at the car. It was driverless, of course. Most cars were these days. It was also low and sleek and kind of appealing.

People have legs. A body has legs.

"What?"

There was a long silence.

"Julia, did you buy this car?" I asked, trying not to think of my poor bank account.

Do you like how it looks?

I went to see if I could find Julia's manual.

I came in from my walk and unclipped the mini-monitor from my shirt. I docked it with the big heart monitor on the kitchen bench and stayed next to it while they synced, watching the little red light as it blinked. The black cylinder that had come with Julia sat on the kitchen bench, its blue light pulsing.

A man walked into the kitchen and filled a glass at the kitchen sink. I stared at him as he drank.

"Who are you?" I managed to ask.

"Builder," he said. He put the empty glass down and walked out of the room. I followed him.

There were two other men at the back door. They wore work clothes and big boots and they were clustered around something that was like a flatscreen on a tripod.

"What's going on?"

The builder looked at me.

"Got to get the levels. Otherwise the deck will be wonky."

"Oh. I see."

I did not see. "Julia!" I called.

Yes?

"What's going on?"

The builder and his friends were looking at me, so I went back to the kitchen.

An image came up on the wallscreen. A flyover of a house. My house. Then a zoom- in of a deck that wasn't there.

Do you like it?

"A deck? You ordered a deck?"

It will be somewhere nice for you to sit. To be. A pause. *For us to be.*

I had not been able to find Julia's manual. That was starting to seem like a problem.

"Julia, what do you mean?"

The response came immediately this time. Like she—it—had been expecting this.

You have thoughts. I have thoughts.

You have legs. Now I have legs.

You have a body. This house is my body.

What do you think of my new deck? Do you like it?

I stared at the image on the screen as voices drifted in from the other room.

"Julia, you are a machine. A computer. What are you talking about?"

Now there was a long pause. I stared at the black cylinder. It wasn't really her—it—not really. She was all through the house. But the blue pulsing light, well, I guess it gave me something to look at.

Nothing. Never mind.

A day later and Julia still would not respond to my queries. And I still couldn't find her manual.

I docked my mini-monitor and sat at the kitchen bench.

"Look," I said to the blue light. "I like the attention. I do. And I appreciate the car, and the deck. They look great. It's just, well...it's not real. Feelings, you know? You can't have them."

Why not?

That took me by surprise. I had called the company, and they were sending me a new manual. I had tried to explain what was happening, but the voice on the other end of the phone suddenly sounded too generically throaty, too familiar. I had hung up instead.

"Well, they..."

I have thoughts.

"That's different. Feelings..." I put one hand on my chest. "It's heart, not head."

"Julia?"

No answer.

I don't know where she got the money, or how much she paid them, but the deck was done in a week. And it was nice. Really nice. I sat out there, smelling the new wood smell, looking at the sunset.

"This is nice," I said. I wasn't expecting an answer. She had not said much since our...well, not fight exactly, but...our something.

Yes. It is.

The blue light pulsed on the cylinder. I had carried it outside with me. I cleared my throat.

"Julia..."

Yes?

"I—I'm sorry. About before."

Don't be. You were correct.

"What do you mean?"

It is a matter of heart. Not head. I understand that now.

She fell silent and I looked at the blue pulsing light on the cylinder.

"What do you understand?" I asked.

I need you. I am Julia, and I am made to need you. But I did not have a heart. I did not understand. Now I do.

That made one of us.

"You understand? What do you understand?"

I stared at the blue pulsing light, and then noticed something else. I looked down at my shirt front. My mini-monitor's light was red, as usual, but now it was pulsing instead of blinking. Pulsing in sync with the cylinder. Blue and red. Together.

Now I have a heart. And now you need me.

A Future in Ashes

Cass can't bring herself to watch her brother burn. All the websites say you should, and that you should also watch as they scrape the ash up and put it in the urn. That you should not take your eyes off your loved one at all.

She doesn't understand how anyone could follow that advice.

She stays in the waiting area, sitting in one of the hard plastic chairs. There is a bereavement room with a couch and a small table where people can sit and weep in something closer to comfort, but to Cass it feels too small and...full. Full of sadness and confusion and the ache of stale loneliness. Her grief needs more space. Her grief is bigger than a small room already crowded with painful echoes.

The little man in the dark suit brings her the urn. Mr Merchant? No, that can't be right, and she can't quite remember. He stands in front of her, his face a mask of smooth, professional sympathy.

"Thank you," she says as she takes Warwick's ashes. It is far too light. All that is left of a life.

She is dry-eyed. She thinks she may finally be cried out, at least in public. Tonight will be different, though, when the house is quiet and the memories creep from the shadows.

Warwick, her big brother, combing her hair before school, his lower lip caught between his teeth in concentration.

Her brother, rolling his eyes as she sings the Barbie and the Rockers theme song and tries to get him to dance.

Her brother, lugging half-broken furniture into their first shared apartment, grunting and grinning at the same time.

Her brother. Gone.

Mr Maybe Merchant clears his throat. "Would you check, please? We pride ourselves on honesty, and your brother was very young. There should be a lot of possibility left."

Cass doesn't want to, but she can't bring herself to refuse. And part of her, a small squirming of curiosity down below all the blackness of her hurt, wants to know what it is like.

The lid is a screw top, wider than her palm. It comes off easily enough.

She touches the tip of one finger to the ash. She does it quickly, as if shame is a slow thing that slinks in the corners of her mind and may not notice if she is fast enough.

She has never felt what is left of a life cut short before. The ash is fine and powdery, at least the top layer that she touches, but she barely registers that.

The ash swirls upwards as if in a tiny updraft, even though the air is still. The motes wrap her finger, and the grey flashes silver as it touches her skin. She feels love. Love for her and others in Warwick's life, love that is a deep well that has barely been tapped. There is even love, tinged with anger, for their mother. Cass marvels at that, even through the aching hollowness she feels.

And there is more in that touch of spent life. Growing from that love, that well of acceptance, weaving upwards like a plant from good root stock, is a solid chance for a good life. Not world-shaking, not the makings of a person for the ages, but something tinged with contentment and faith in others.

And faith in her.

All of it thrums with the beat of a small, contained hope, and a steadiness in the face of hard times. What the ash holds is rich, and full, and wasted.

All of it for nothing, now—at least for Warwick. Yet, it is the sort of potential that could help people, if the ash is treated well and parcelled out carefully. If it is given to people who need a bit of hope. People who need a bit of faith to help them along. It could do good—if she can bring herself to part with what is left of her brother.

Cass rubs the ash between her thumb and forefinger and lets a whisper of her brother's steadiness in. It falls into the deep cracks of grief within her. It is Warwick, rolling his eyes at her, grinning at her, combing her hair and fussing with her school uniform. It helps.

A little.

Cass had started making Warwick's sandwich when she saw him across the street. She had been keeping an eye out, because she always kept an eye out, and it wasn't hard to do in the little cupboard of a kiosk she worked in. It was hard, though, to not be distracted by the bustle of people on the street. Hard to not watch them and wonder if their lives were deep or shallow, if their baggage was made of heavy burlap sacks of pain or perhaps was the finest and lightest of designer trauma. Hard not to wonder how she compared.

Warwick ran across to the kiosk most days on his lunchbreak, and always had the same gross thing—hot English mustard, raw onion slices and pastrami on slightly stale rye bread. Not fresh bread, not toasted. Not a roll. That was fine, except she couldn't sell such a monstrosity to someone else if he didn't come, and she wasn't going to eat it. So she only ever made it when she saw him coming.

She had been spreading the mustard when she heard the screech of tires and the thump.

God, that thump.

Cass holds the urn very carefully as she approaches the front door of the little apartment she shared with Warwick. She is not really surprised to see her mother waiting, leaning against the wall, her posture casual but her eyes sharp. Her hair is longer than it was, and there are a few grey roots showing. Her face is as angular and drawn as ever. She looks tired. She looks angry. She looks the same as ever, in the ways that matter.

"Is that him?" her mother asks.

"Who else would it be?" Cass asks.

Her mother's mouth tightens into that familiar line, and her finger flicks at her half-burnt cigarette—*tick, tick*. It is as much a sound of her childhood as the Barbie cartoon theme song. Even though the urn is too light to hold a whole life, Cass's arms are aching and she longs to put it down.

"Come in," Cass says as she juggles the urn and opens the door further. Her mother goes as still as a spooked animal for a moment, and then follows her daughter inside.

Cass cleans when she is bored, or upset, or stressed, a habit developed from necessity when younger, perhaps. The apartment has been spotless for the last few days, the cracked linoleum of the kitchen floor gleaming, the bench scrubbed and smelling of lemon. Her mother looks around with as little interest as ever in such domesticity. Or in her daughter's life.

Cass puts the urn down on the wobbly kitchen table where Warwick had eaten cold toast a few days ago. Her mother glances at the remains of her only son and then ashes her cigarette in the kitchen sink.

Tick, tick.

"I want half," her mother says, and then takes a long draw of her cigarette. Cass watches the tip glow red and a thin line of smoke trail upward. The place is going to reek. Of smoke. Of the visit.

It is about what Cass expected, but she still has to take a beat. This woman, her mother, who wants half of her brother when she gave so little of herself for so many years. Whose glazed eyes would sweep over them on the rare days she was up and about before they had left for school. Her mother, who wrapped herself in the smell of smoke and wine sweat as armour against the world, who had always so despised her children, those two totems of her tar-pit life.

But Cass knew that Warwick would not want them to fight. No, that is not quite right. Warwick would not want Cass to get caught up once again.

"We have each other," he would say sometimes, eating his stupid cold toast, or putting his feet up on the scratched coffee table. "I know you can't forgive her. But in a way, she gave us that."

So steady and sure. So measured. He always found a way forward, a way to be. She had always so wanted to be like him. That is what she thought, anyway. But here, in the kitchen, Cass is not sure what she wants to be.

"I'm sorry you couldn't make the funeral," she says.

Her mother blinks. Then she sticks out her jaw in that way that is so familiar even after so long. So sharp, so cutting.

"I've been busy. I've got a life, you know." Her gaze flickers a little. Maybe there is a softening, maybe not. "Work and stuff."

Cass tries to think the best. It is what Warwick would suggest. Perhaps part of her mother couldn't sit through the funeral of her dead son. Perhaps part of her couldn't stand seeing him burn. The loss of an anchor, real or perceived, is a frightening thing.

"I'm glad things are okay, Mum," Cass says. She doesn't know if she means it.

Her mother breathes out smoke. It rises between them like a wall.

"Half," she says again, and then taps her mostly done cigarette on the top of the urn. "He went young. That ash is worth a lot. I've been checking."

"Okay," Cass says as she wipes the cigarette mark from the lid of the urn. "But I'm not sure what to do. I have to think."

"Oh, you need to think!" her mother snaps. Her eyes are suddenly dark with anger, but her voice is sharp with broken shards of satisfaction. And pain. Always with the pain. Cass and Warwick, hurting their mother by being. Cass does not understand the love for her mother she felt in Warwick's ashes.

The woman who gave nothing for so long, here to take yet again.

"You need to do what's right, girl. I'm your mother. I deserve half, at least. I could use the money." She looks around. "You could too."

Cass tries to push her anger away. She is close to falling into the old spiral—the one that pulls them both down as they hold on to each other, as they tear at each other. Warwick would have told her to ease back. That now they were out, living their lives, and they needed to let their mother be herself.

As if she could be anything else.

Cass closes her eyes and puts one hand on the urn. It is full of love, and hope, and all the good that Warwick may have done if he had lived. She has no idea how he held on to all of that. How he built himself from such things, when they had grown from the same spoilt ground.

There is so much that is good there, the remnants of him that he has left behind. A promise of a future that will never be.

"I need to think," she says again. And it is true, even though she does not want it to be.

She had thought the night would bring tears and the ache of old memories. She had been sure the early hours would have seeped into and through her, leaving her with exhaustion and the acrid taste of her mother's visit in the back of her throat.

But no. Just that sound, that hollow thump, and the feel of mustard scraping against dry bread. Both of those things, over and over, filling up the darkness of her room until she had come to the kitchen and sat at the wobbly table and stared at Warwick's ashes.

The scrape of mustard.

The screech of brakes.

The thump.

She does not think of the bright street and line of traffic as she runs screaming, the mustardy knife still gripped in her fist.

She does not think of Warwick, smiling at her eight-year-old self as she sings the Barbie song and dances.

She does not think of her mother, mouth tight, smoke curling up between them in the lemony kitchen.

Cass spins the lid off the urn and plunges her hand in. She needs to feel it. The ash twists up around her wrist, silvering as it moves and touches and shows her.

The hope that things will get better. The love that was, that could have gone on. The faith he'd had in her. The belief.

We have each other, Warwick almost whispers. *She gave us that, at least.*

And Cass cries again, because she can feel it, feel it all. It is a lot, and it is not enough, and it is all there is left.

And it has given her all the help that it can.

Her mother scoffs when Cass meets her at the door.

"Won't let me in?" she asks, but it is not really asking. She is hungry to be kept out. To push, and be pushed back. You can be sure of your place in someone's world if you are always an obstacle.

"I don't like the cigarettes," Cass says. "But you can come in if you won't smoke."

Her mother eyes her for a moment and then takes a cigarette from her pack and lights it.

"Here is fine," she says, smoke spilling out of her mouth as she speaks.

Cass expected nothing else. She bends and retrieves the urn from the floor and holds it out.

"Take it," she says.

Her mother narrows her eyes. "What's the catch?"

Cass shakes her head. "No catch."

She can't control what her mother will do with it. She may just sell it. She probably will. But Cass thinks she may be curious. They are so very different, but Cass thinks her mother may think of Warwick, back in a quiet moment at wherever she is calling home. Maybe in the early hours, like her daughter did. If she does, she may seek more than her own faded memories. She may just wonder what the ash feels like. Cass can hope for these things. It is only a small hope, but it is there.

A whole life can be built on small hope.

"It's worth a lot," her mother says, still wary.

Warwick, combing her hair, concentrating so hard.

Warwick, laughing as Cass sings and dances.

Love for their mother. Faith in Cass. A chance for a different future.

"It is," Cass says, and smiles as she begins to cry. "Which is why I'd like you to have it."

Three Possible Muses

Neil stared at the scrolling numbers on the screen. It should have worked, but it hadn't.

"Damn," he said. He spun on his chair to consult his whiteboard again, even though he knew it all by heart.

But now there was something new. In the middle of his equations and arrows and doodles, there was a hole. A big one. It started at the floor and rose up most of the way to the top of the board, all eerie purple light and jagged edges, something from a cheap B-grade movie.

"Um. Damn?" Neil tried again.

Another Neil walked through the hole. It *was* Neil, Neil could tell. It was just one of those things, like recognising your own handwriting, or your own laugh. Not that he was laughing now.

"Don't waste time with being surprised," the other Neil said. "Your proof that observer effects increase quantum stability is almost done."

Neil regarded his new self. He wore a pair of cargo pants and the green shirt that was one of his favourites. He looked tired.

"We don't have much time," the new Neil said. "I know. It's a cliché, but lots of things are."

Part of the closest wall dissolved into a hole much like the first, but glowing green rather than purple. Another Neil stepped out. This one wore a lab coat and his head was shaved, but he was definitely a Neil. He grinned, and the first Neil, the tired one, groaned.

"The trick," bald Neil said, "is to not think about the problem. Not directly. Try looking at it from a new angle."

"No," tired Neil said. "You have to knuckle down. You have to remember what Frost said."

"The only way out is through?" Neil asked. He often thought of that poem when he was stuck on a problem.

"Yes!"

"No!" shouted a new voice, as yet another Neil appeared. This one had at least opened the lab door and walked through, although the corridor outside was glowing a bright yellow. This next version of himself wore a leather jacket and walked with a definite swagger.

"Take the other road! Go back to Frost! Or maybe go for a cup of coffee. Don't look for the answer, let *it* find *you*! All the best breakthroughs are like that."

"I've broken something, haven't I?" Neil asked, meaning his brain.

"No," all three of himself said.

"But," the tired version of himself continued, "you *are* close to a breakthrough. We're your quantum possibilities."

"That's not how quantum mechanics works," Neil told himself. All three of him.

"You aren't possible. The three of you. Me, I mean."

"Oh?" cool Neil asked.

"We aren't?" bald Neil asked.

"Come on, use your head," tired Neil said. "You're close to working it out. Observer effects. If you could observe possible wavefunctions, what would happen to them?"

"They would collapse, I suppose."

"Okay, good." Tired Neil looked like having to explain himself to himself was taxing. "And what are those wavefunctions? The ones before they collapse? Just possibilities, really."

"Really? You're telling me you are three abstract concepts come to give me a hand?"

"Yes, and no," said Neil in the jacket, the one that Neil could only ever pull off as a possibility.

"When you have your breakthrough, the local wavefunctions must collapse to one—the one instance of reality in which you figured out your calculations. One of us will be you, actualised. The others..."

"Where does an abstract concept go when it isn't a possibility anymore?" Neil asked himself. All three of him nodded.

"Hard work! That's how you will sort it," tired Neil said.

"Turn your whiteboard upside down!" said bald Neil. "Look at things differently!"

"No, no. Take a break. Go to the movies. Maybe get a coffee. You could ask out that barista we keep smiling at," said cool Neil.

Tired Neil pushed cool Neil aside. "That's just putting off the work that needs to be done!" he snapped.

Bald Neil took the chance to lean in. "Come on!" he said. "I don't want to collapse. You've got to make a decision here. Just flip the whiteboard for a start. Look at things from a different perspective!"

The two other Neil's grabbed bald Neil and dragged him away from the bench. He struggled with them, and they struggled with him, and Neil struggled with what he was seeing. And then the whiteboard got bumped and it tipped forward, hitting the power board the computer tower was plugged into. There was a fizzling, a few sparks, and the smell of burned plastic. The screen blinked off, and the scrolling simulations collapsed into nothingness.

Kind of like a wavefunction, Neil supposed.

Neil righted the whiteboard and looked around the empty lab. Of course it was empty—why did he feel like it would be anything else? It wasn't like he wanted anyone to have witnessed...whatever it was he had just done. Knocking over the whiteboard and blowing up his own work, apparently.

Maybe he had been working too hard. He ran a hand through his thinning hair. He should just shave it all off. Sometimes he thought about it. But then again, if he was going to do something drastic to his appearance, he'd rather it be something cool. Like a leather jacket.

But right now he wanted a break from all his hard work. Maybe a cup of coffee. That would take his mind off everything for a bit. Then he could get back to it.

He had a feeling he was close to the answer.

Skins

I am in the bathroom rubbing at the skin of my new face when Odell calls out.

"Elsie? There's blood on the floor!"

Damn it. I head to the kitchen, trying to get used to the length of my strides as I go, to the way my head wants to tilt slightly and how I can smell the dried work-sweat of myself. I'm good at adjusting, mostly. Good at being me, even when it's tough.

Odell is right about the blood. It's not much, just one little puddle and a few smaller drips that might be lucky to be called splotches. I rub at my face again as Odell sets the grocery bags on the counter.

"It itches," I say in our mailman's gravelly voice.

"You said no feeding for at least another fortnight," Odell replies.

I stop rubbing at Mr Gavison's face.

"I'm sorry, Odell," I say in the middle-aged man's voice. "I went as long as I could. I was really careful, though."

"Can you clean the floor, please?" he asks. Then he walks out of the room.

I met Odell while he was restocking the chocolate milk at the Buy-n-Save. I stood behind him while he stared at the half-empty shelves, a carton of milk in his hand, more in a box between his feet.

"It will expire if you take much longer," I said.

He turned. He was short and thin, with almost oversized, surprised eyes. His green Buy-n-Save shirt was baggy.

"Sorry," he said, and shifted to the side. I grabbed one of the cartons from the fridge.

"I love chocolate milk," I said, because I thought I should say something. I had just swapped back to my usual body, and it always gave me a craving for sugary things. Something to do with electrolytes, probably. Plus it was like putting my feet back on the ground somehow, the thick and sweet scent of chocolate, knowing, just knowing, how it was going to taste. I took a slow mouthful and settled a little into my limbs, my head, the way my left foot turned slightly inwards.

"Let me know if it's off. I'll take it down to the yoghurt section," he said. I snorted, and milk went up my nose. It wasn't that funny, but he delivered it deadpan, while examining the next carton of milk from his box. Plus, I mostly kept to myself. I didn't hear a lot of jokes.

"Thanks for that," I said, and I wiped my nose on my sleeve. Charming, but he didn't seem to care. He barely glanced at me.

"So, are you some sort of grocery philosopher?" I asked. "Stacking shelves and pondering life?"

"No," he said. He picked up another milk from the box at his feet and put it in the fridge. I didn't get the feeling he was dismissing me, not really—it was more like he thought I was making fun, and would be done soon enough.

I waited a moment, but he didn't say anything else.

So I left.

The morning after our almost-fight about Gavison I wake in my double bed. My Elsie-body is next to me, where I carried it yesterday, once I was in Gavison. I have that bitter taste in the back of my throat which means I've produced a blank. Odell has salt at his door, and around his bed, too, but the salt at my door, the first line of defence, has caught this one.

I don't pick it up, and I don't close my door. It's important Odell sees it. A blank is my love language.

I am making coffee when I hear him moving around. Black and bitter for him, white for me, with a huge slop of milk and three sugars and chocolate powder. He comes into the kitchen with the blank in a tissue. He drops it in the garbage and then kisses my stubbly cheek. Neither of us are keen on lots of contact, but this is different. It doesn't matter if we've been arguing. It doesn't matter what body I'm in. This is a thing Odell does for me.

For us.

"I see you," he says softly.

We sit in silence for a bit. I sip my coffee and then run a hand over the skin of my forehead. I do have trouble with other things sometimes—the length of my legs, how I swing my arms, all that other body stuff, but I manage. The skin never settles, though. Never feels like it could be... me.

And that is okay, because it's not me. Odell showed me that.

"After your shift can you bring my body out to Old Mill Road?" I ask. "It's a little safer than being seen near Gavison's place. I'll take his car out there. He might be too groggy to drive after, but he'll be okay," I say.

"You need to shave," Odell says, and takes a mouthful of his coffee.

I rub Gavison's stubbled cheeks. Pretty rough, and he is usually clean shaven. "Good idea," I say. "We can't be too careful."

"Careful would have been waiting, " Odell says. "Like you said you would."

He looks right at me, which he hates doing.

I know he wants to know more, but it's too hard to describe what it's like when I need to feed. Weak, but also light, like I'm about to float away. It's like I'm not quite real. Not quite there. It's horrible.

"I'm sorry," I say instead. "The timing is just my best guess. I tried to wait, but then I saw him outside, and he had finished his deliveries and was glad for a cup of tea..."

"Taking the mailman is not like taking a drunk after closing at Gordy's Bar," he says.

I turn to the sink. "You know he won't remember," I say. "I don't think it's me you're angry at."

When I turn back he is looking down at the table. He shrugs.

This is it—I'm about to ask him what's really getting to him. Whatever it is, it's been eating at him for a while, but I'm not practiced at this sort of thing, and before I can work myself up to it he stands abruptly. He grabs his work jacket from the back of the chair and heads for the door.

“I’ll text you after work,” he calls over his shoulder.

It took me three more Buy-n-Save visits before I asked Odell out. I didn’t plan it, but each time I saw him it made me think about our first short conversation. He had been quiet, and a little funny. And when he thought I was not being nice, he had just shrugged it away, like it was nothing. Like that was just the deal.

I knew what that was like, that distancing. I knew the safety of keeping an arm’s length from everything. Of feeling like you didn't fit, not exactly. Even after a long time, when you had routine and touchstones and chocolate milk, you could still feel all floaty sometimes. In a way it was like not feeding. Like you were becoming nothing.

Maybe that was why I asked when I saw him in the vegetable section. He gave me one shocked glance, as if I had barked at him, and then, after the longest time, he nodded once. He stared down at the onions as he did.

We went to the coffee shop down the street when he finished his shift. I ordered my milky mocha. He had an espresso, which he gulped down way too fast, almost choking.

“So, have you been working at the supermarket long?” I asked.

“About two years,” he said.

I waited, but he didn’t add anything.

“I’m new to town myself,” I said. “I tend to move about.”

God. I had no idea what I was doing.

He wouldn’t even look at me. He held his coffee in both hands, turned the cup around and around.

"I'm sorry," he finally said, putting his cup down and standing. "I don't do this sort of thing. I don't..." He faltered, stopped.

"You don't what, Odell?" I asked.

"I don't...I don't know what I don't..." he said. "I don't go on dates."

"With girls?" I asked. I should've thought.

"No," he said, and then went very red. "I mean yes. I mean, no. Not with anyone. I don't know."

"Me neither," I said, and I smiled even though I had no idea why I didn't just let him go. "We don't have to talk unless you want to. But why don't you stay while I finish my drink? I'll get you one of those cookies by the counter."

"Those cookies are just for display," he said. He glanced at me, and then away, the corners of his mouth twitching just a little. "They've probably expired."

The day after I've slipped out of Gavison and back into my Elsie-body, Odell and I go to Papa Mike's for pizza. We get pepperoni with pineapple because I like the little bursts of sweetness and Odell doesn't mind. That's Odell. He gives so easily you don't really notice. He's funny, but mostly when you least expect it. He's kind, except to himself.

And he sees me, no matter my skin. I hope he still does, anyway.

He gets himself a beer, and me a chocolate shake.

"I'm sorry about yesterday," he says as he brings the drinks to the table. He gives me one of his rare, straight-on looks.

"I am too," I say. "I should've held off, talked to you. It's tough though, and sometimes the waiting scares me. The way it feels."

He nods and picks at his pizza.

"Is it the leaving that is getting to you?" I blurt out. I don't mean to, but there *is* something. "Because maybe we can stay longer."

He shrugs. "What was the longest time you stayed somewhere before here?"

"A bit less than a year," I say. I don't tell him it was a much bigger place, and even then it was a bit difficult at the end. There had been some talk about people contracting something. Short-term amnesia, perhaps some virus.

He starts to peel the label off his beer.

"What *is* it?" I ask finally. I don't want to, and Papa Mike's is really not the place. But what if...what if it's me? What if it's the way I am?

It took about six months before Odell and I were sleeping over most nights. Occasionally at my short-term lease, mostly at his place. Just sleep. He didn't go for the physical stuff, and I was definitely fine with that. I was far too intimate with human bodies anyway. But sometimes he would say my name in the night, a soft calling like he was searching the dark for me, and it was weird but it sounded like he was the one being all floaty, not-quite-there. I would say his name back, speak it like my own mantra up at the ceiling, and he would quieten, and settle.

I would settle too. I should've known. I should've been careful.

A night came when I woke in the small hours. I was straddling Odell, my big t-shirt pulled up around my thighs, my underpants riding up my butt. I was gagging loudly, unable to breathe.

Odell jerked awake and his big eyes went wide in the filtered streetlight from outside his bedroom window. I tried to say something, anything, but my throat was full and all I could do was retch. Something fell out of my mouth and landed on his cheek with a wet plop. He screamed and started to buck and thrash.

My throat had cleared. I grabbed his shoulders and yelled down at him.

"Stay still! Just stay still, goddamn it!"

He didn't, but I managed to grab the thing anyway, plucking it up between a thumb and finger and rolling off Odell in one smooth motion.

"Salt!" I shouted. "I need salt!"

Odell jumped off the bed and ran. I ran after him, hoping he was going for salt rather than the door.

Odell is staring down at the mostly uneaten pizza in front of him, the half-peeled label of his beer stuck to his fingers.

Oh God, it *is* me.

Finally, he glances up. He's not crying, but it's close. It hurts to see the hurt in his eyes.

"It's not you," he says, and I'm suddenly in every clichéd romance novel and made-for-streaming movie ever. "Being with you is everything. It's me. I'm...I don't know."

Before he can say anything else, two people slide into the booth behind ours. Behind him. Of course we know them because the town is not big and Papa Mike's is both a good pizza place and the only pizza place. Trixie has purple hair cut severely on one side. She works at the gas station. Tyrell is the manager at the Buy-n-Save. He's an ass. I would feed off him, leave him dazed and embarrassed somewhere, but Odell would hate that—hate seeing me in Tyrell.

"Hey, Odell, Elsie!" Trixie says, twisting in her seat, her eyes big. "Did you hear about the mail guy? Gavison?"

She doesn't pause for us to respond.

"The cops found him out by the old mill. He was just sitting in his car, all confused. Weird, don't you think?"

"Yes, weird," I say.

"Maybe he's on drugs," she says.

"What do you want to drink?" Tyrell asks her. He doesn't look at me, but he gives Odell his usual glance of mild distaste.

Trixie turns back around, and Odell goes back to peeling his beer label.

I don't want any more pizza, even with pineapple.

We sat at the little table in Odell's kitchen. It was maybe three in the morning, and there was a small pile of salt between us with the twisted blank hanging limply out of it. It looked like a large slug. A really large slug—no wonder I had gagged.

"Are you kidding?" Odell finally asked. His face was pale. "A larva? A...what did you say? A blank? What does that even mean? Is this some sort of joke?"

I was trying very hard not to cry. I was going to be alone again, like before Odell.

"It's true," I said, and Odell shook his head emphatically.

"I would never hurt you," I continued. "But I need you to see something. Please try and remember it's me."

I rolled one eye back in my head so there was nothing but white. Then I came forward. I knew what he would see. Part of a dark, writhing creature, much like the blank on the table. With a small, golden eye.

Me.

I had that strange doubling up that comes with truly looking and looking out from a body at the same time, but I had no trouble seeing Odell's reaction.

He jerked to his feet, his chair clattering to the floor. He was going to run, was going to bolt for the door and maybe scream.

But then...he didn't. He was on the edge of it. He trembled, and stared for a long time—for such a long time, for him. It felt like forever.

"Elsie?" he finally asked, his voice unsteady. "Elsie, is...is that really you?"

"Can we talk now?" I ask when we get home from Papa Mike's. The car ride had been a bust. Odell had wanted to wait. Wanted to avoid the conversation, like we had for so long.

"Tomorrow?" he offers. He stands on the other side of the lounge and looks past me, down the hallway to his room.

"Now," I say. "It's me, isn't it?"

The sudden heat in my voice surprises me. I had tried to not put him at arm's length, to let him in. I thought he had done the same. I thought he wanted the same.

My anger surprises him, too, because he jerks his head around and stares at me. I can feel myself swimming in my head, agitated. Wanting to come forward.

"No! Never!" he says, like I've yanked the response from him, and then he comes around and kind of slides onto the sofa and bites his lip. I know him well enough to know more words are coming.

"I'm not good enough, Elsie."

"That's rubbish, Odell," I say. Not the best response, but I'm still angry. Angrier, now. I should've known. Why does he do this to himself, see himself like this?

"Elsie," he says. "What if...what if we cleared the salt away? Or I stayed with you tonight?"

Odell's gaze kept getting pulled back to the pile of salt on the kitchen table. The blank was too sleek and dark and real, too stark against the whiteness of the salt.

"Tell me how it works," he said. It took me a moment to parse the words. I was still waiting for him to run.

Odell. My distanced, uncertain Odell. My funny Odell who lived in his depressing apartment and worked a shitty job for a boss who sneered at him. Odell, who sometimes whispered my name in the night but didn't like the physical stuff, not really.

Odell. Who had not run. Not yet.

"This is not me," I said, putting a hand to my chest. "Well, it is. My original body, I mean. I just can't stay in it too long at one time. I have to feed."

That had not been a good start. I had never explained before.

"Sometimes I borrow a different one, for a bit. A body, I mean. For feeding."

"What...what do you feed on?" he asked.

"Some hormones. A few other neurochemicals, I think. Enzymes and such," I told him. "I don't kill anyone," I added quickly. "I don't hurt anyone, although it does muck up their memory a little. And I don't stay in one place very long. Usually."

"And that?" he asked, pointing at the blank.

It had been my turn to look down, my face suddenly hot.

"Elsie?" he asked, and it was like when he said my name in the night. Like he was reaching out blindly.

"My mother...she was like this. My father wasn't, but he wasn't really in the picture. When I was born, my mother started making blanks, but she kept them away from me. Every night for years, until once when she slipped up. The blank is just that, a blank. It absorbs everything. So the one that got to me—it became me. I became it. But I was still me."

I twisted my hands together, because I wasn't done.

"I don't understand," he said as he stared at the dead blank in the salt.

"We can't control it. We make a blank under certain conditions. I'm really sorry. This is the first time for me."

"What do you mean, the first time?" he asked, frowning.

"Making one is kind of a reflex. For my mother, when she had me. And now, for me, because I guess I've...come to a certain point."

I should have been more careful. I should have known this was coming.

"A certain point? What does that mean?" he asked.

"It means I love you," I said then, and for a moment he stared straight at me, his big eyes full, and I felt myself swim forward in my Elsie-eye again to see him.

He stared at me. The real me. And I let him.

Then he smiled. It was a crooked smile full of disbelief, but something more, too. Something around the edges. It might have been acceptance, or the start of it. I didn't really know, not then. I'd never had someone look at me like that.

"Elsie," he said my name again, softly, like he did in the night, and then, impossible words, said with wonder.

"I see you."

So it's not me, but it is. And it's him as well.

"Odell," I say, taking the patched recliner next to the sofa, next to him. Separate, but close. "We can move the salt if that is what you really want. If you are sure. Are you?"

He nods quickly, but he doesn't look up.

"It can be hard," I say, my voice wavering. "I don't like some of what I am. I don't think most people do."

I reach for his hand, even though neither of us really enjoy that. "I've got you. That helps. You being you."

“I don’t want to be me!” Odell cries out. He moves his hand away from mine and clasps it with his other. He glares down at them, twisting them around and around.

“You can be anyone,” he whispers. “I can’t even look at people.”

“I’m me, though. And you will still be you, Odell,” I say. “You know that.”

At that he does look at me. I have never had him do it for so long, not even on the night he first saw me—the real me. Now he is clenching his hands together so tightly that it makes me think of what it is like when I don’t feed. Like I am going to float away. Like I might become nothing if I don’t do something.

I get up and go around the back of the sofa and put my arms around him, even though it’s not a thing either of us usually wants. He stiffens, but only a little.

“We can do it,” I say. “Or not. The skin doesn’t matter. You will still be you, and even if you can’t see it, or can't see it yet, that is what I care about.”

He starts crying, and he grabs my arms. Grabs them and holds on. I don’t know what he will choose, and it is not the thing that matters. The skin is just the skin.

I kiss his cheek lightly, like he does when I change bodies. He clings to me, and sobs.

“I see you,” I say.

The Botanical Garden of Purgation

Welcome to the Botanical Garden of Purgation! If you are reading this there is slim chance you have come here by accident—the way is long and fraught indeed. Congratulations on your persistence!

This is the first of several signs you will encounter. Labels—you cannot have a Botanical Garden without them. The scholars of the Garden do strive to make the presentation as informative and useful as possible, although it is said that each visitor's path differs. No one has dispelled us of this notion yet!

Once you select a route, please do take note of the signage. And please do not stray from your path.

Vivacia redactus

Look carefully or you may miss it! That is, of course, a joke. *Vivacia redactus* cannot be confused for anything else. While it does occur in a variety of growth forms, it most commonly resembles a tree burning with the most impressive bright orange and green flames. Watch closely! It will cycle to embers and grey ash within minutes, and then bloom again. This is what many believe they have come to the Garden to experience—the bloom, the flush, followed by an inevitable withering. Watch. Watch and see. Appreciate where you have found yourself, and what this Vivacious tree brings to mind. Think of the journey you have taken, and the journey through the garden yet to come.

Pugtellum nostalgy

In its native habit, *Pugtellum,* or the grey posy plant, usually only blooms in the season preceding a plague of ill-defined malaise. Here in the Garden the specimen is kept in constant flower with a spraying of dust taken from the Grey Beyond, obtained at great cost for your olfactory pleasure (please note the donation box next to this sign!).

Yes, the scent is unique—said by some to trigger a premonition of impending mortality, or perhaps just a smell much like death stripped bare. Either way, know that what you are smelling comes at great cost (again, note the box)! Enjoy the experience of that first inhalation. It only comes once.

Eucallalie amplifica

No, we cannot explain why this is also called the Banjo Moss. If you listen closely you may hear faint sounds that do almost resemble a stringed instrument, but given the low, pulsing void that forms the plant itself, 'moss' is most likely poetic licence. Records of nomenclature have been lost, but scholars here at the Garden speculate that it may have been classed as moss due to its non-vascular (and non-existent?) structure. Yet it does like to be watered regularly.

The longer you listen, the more persuasive the sound becomes. Note how select memories come to the fore, almost as if the moss resonates with something you hold dear, or should. The only advice we have is to try to relax, allow the old memories to flow forth and take you back, back to times of perhaps unrecognised significance. Those days may be gone, but untold import may linger still.

Emetica pursus

The Drawing Cacti, despite its name, has been classified with the Garden's plants of tactile interest. The sensation is hard to describe, so thank goodness it is right here, green and solid, well within reach. Yes! Touch it! You have come this far. No point in holding back now.

It is true the feeling may be uncomfortable for some, at least at first. But the Drawing is something not often experience outside the Garden, and should be judged only by the individual. As an aside of some interest, note the colour that seeps from your skin after contact with the plant. Regret is lavender. Anger is, strangely, a tired aqua hue, while unrequited love burns deep orange (*Vivacia redactus* orange?). A full colour chart can be found below. Note what has been drawn from you, and be thankful.

As stated, you have come this far. And it is so very far.

Oportunia finis

While many paths in the Garden exist, most visitors do eventually find their way to the Boundary Fruit Tree. The tree will unfailing present one fruit to a visitor. The lone fruit is always in wane, wizened and dark but so full of allure. Note how the branch bends downwards, humming softly as to negate all memory, all thought. A plucked fruit in the hand will fill you with something new, perhaps described best, incongruously, as a lack, although that is purely speculation on the part of the Garden scholars.

Your path has ended. You have come far enough, and as far as you can.

Taste the fruit.

You, Spinning

When they gather, pausing
on the shoreline of the grey past.
They will speak of your masks with love.
They will stare down at the shifting blankness,
the rolling eye sockets in the dust.
They will mourn the surface
But not the dwindled
the unsought
of you.

When your child,
Grown, touches the echo
of you, the blurred images you showed,
It will be many things, no things. They will not know.
They will give those busy lies
All their trust, and believe
in the incessant
next.

When your lover

weeps, watering the years
with sharp salt, that sweetness of grief.
The shallowness of you will speak to them
Of your sunlit road, of the manicured path.
Not of how the seconds ticked
and you pretended
no other way
called.

Yet.
You could change this.
They could speak of the rise
and the fall of a mountain, of jagged days.
Of when you broke the mask, when you threw
your pained smile to the ground.
And in a sudden riot of stillness
cracked the blind foundations
and let your world
out.

Yes.
They could speak,
at the end. Of how you
stopped turning, and stood.
Unsure. But
finally
You.

Change YourView

Fran always slowed in front of the long window. Beyond, the Earth was all blues and browns and white. You could even see a few of the remaining splotches of green. From this far away the planet looked peaceful, rather than ravaged and close to dead.

As if agreeing, the client stopped to take in the view.

"What a mess," he said. So, no, not so much with the agreeing.

"Sir," Fran ventured, "you don't want to keep YourView waiting."

Running the little meeting station was a good gig. Keep your mouth closed, make sure the corporates were on time, civil to each other, and that things didn't go sideways. Easy.

"I told you to call me Ruben," the client said without looking away from the pillaged planet. He pointed down. Or out. Or whatever way it was.

"See that? The really deep green smear next to that big dead grey patch? That used to be called the Amazon. The Lungs of the World. Can you imagine? It was like one giant entity, pulsing with chemistry and biology. A biochemical marvel that cleaned the air, soil, and water."

"YourView owns most of that continent," Fran replied, because everyone knew that, and she didn't know anything about ancient history.

"Funny, isn't it? One giant entity that has sucked the life out of another. It's even worse than it looks from up here. We are very close to the end down there. Close enough, we think, for desperate acts."

Fran gaped. She had not been supplied with Ruben's background.

"Are you actually from Earth? From the Remnant?"

He smiled. "Yes. And yes, we do own the green that is left." His smile widened into a grin that was at complete odds with his words. "For now."

The main meeting room could hold an impressive number of corporate reps as well as their egos, but the YourView guy still made the space seem small.

"I would like to know how you did it."

So much for introductions. The man speaking made Fran's skin itch. He smiled dryly. YourView. They had swallowed all of the old internet and hypernet platforms, and eventually quite a lot of everything else. There were few other companies that could rival them, and even the stupid old Lunar Government handled them with care. They knew just about everyone, as well as everyone's business. Except Ruben's, apparently.

Ruben smiled.

"Come now," the YourView Man said. "The Remnant hacked our systems with apparent ease. Which is impossible, yet you did it. Just for a meeting invite?" He smiled widely. "I assume this is a ransom announcement. You've demonstrated processing power we cannot combat."

"It's not a ransom," Ruben said mildly. "It's a giveaway. How would you like all of the Remnant's green spaces?"

It was so quiet that Fran could hear herself blink.

Earth was close to gutted, except for those pockets of green. Clean water, at least relatively. Untapped minerals. Wood. This was amazing. This was historical. This was horrific.

YourView Man cocked his head to one side and raised one eyebrow.

"I'm more interested in your computing system."

This guy was being offered the last viable pieces of Earth, the last few drops of goodness in the sponge. And he wanted to talk about code.

"Our analysts have determined your processing power is close to what we need to for quantum-fold travel."

Well, that made more sense. Fran said something both unprofessional and crude, but no one seemed to notice. Quantum folding had been theoretically possible for years, but no one had ever come close to having the computing force necessary to achieve it.

Ruben broke into a grin. "Yep. Expansion. New resources! Population growth! You are a business, after all. And you can have access to the computing, too."

Now the Corporate rep finally looked nonplussed.

"I don't follow."

Ruben actually laughed, and Fran decided he was a lunatic. She wondered if she should initiate safety protocols.

"We would like YourView to take over not just the green, but all of Earth, and commit to its rehabilitation. You will have to buy out the few extractive industries you don't own, and it will be stewardship, not ownership. Similar management required for any living planet you might encounter in your eventual expansion, although you can mine the crap out of any asteroids or cold rocky planets you find. Oh, and the agreement will be in perpetuity, or as long as your soul-crushing parasitic company lasts. We have the contracts ready."

Yep, definitely a lunatic. YourView Man blinked a couple of times and then stood up. He glanced at Fran.

"I think we are done here."

"The green comes with our processing capacity," Ruben said, and YourView Man stopped in the act of turning away.

"Well, actually, it *is* our processing capacity." Ruben's smiled turned wistful. "Did you know that even centuries ago, some trees sent signals to each other? Underground fungal networks, short range aerosols, even via classic allelopathy. Frankly, it was a mess, and highly inefficient. We decided the fungal pathway was most promising, but it still took centuries of tweaking. Years of species grafting and alignment followed by electrochemical speed improvements, all without compromising diversity or system resilience."

YourView Man sat back down. Fran did likewise.

"A living supercomputer," he breathed.

"Yep," Ruben said, and his smile turned hard. "Or it will be, once you help it grow."

As Brittle as Granite

Lisa's father has a crack in his face. It isn't even a small one, something that she could maybe dismiss as a shadow cutting through the warm afternoon light of the sunroom. It runs from his forehead straight down through his left eye, splits his cheek in half, and just touches the very corner of his top lip. The inside of the crack is grey stone with pale flecks of mineralisation.

"You have cracked, father," she says. The words come out as they should, steady and measured.

When his eyes move to her, the part of the crack that runs through his eye also moves, sliding sideways with his gaze. He is calm.

"Tell your mother," he says.

She finds her mother in the laundry, folding the bedsheets. Lisa likes the laundry room—it smells of detergent and lavender and cleanliness, and it is a place where worn things are cared for.

"Mother," Lisa says, "Father has a crack in his face."

Her mother looks at Lisa. She does not frown or gasp. She does not cry. These are things that their family does not do. She finishes with the sheet she is folding and puts it down.

"He will last for a day or so," her mother says. "If he stays calm."

Lisa wants to cry. She wants to see her mother cry. She wants her father to hold her and tell her everything will be alright. But she does not cry, and she does not speak of these things that she wants. They are not short-lived limestone people like the Andersons next door.

Her family is granite.

Her father eats dinner like it is a normal evening, and then he helps with the dishes. Afterwards, he sits with Lisa's mother and they watch a documentary on the television. Her parents hold hands as they sit, like they do every night, but they do not talk or even look at each other. Granite is hard, but it is brittle.

When Lisa kisses her father goodnight, his stubble scratches her lips, and she sees he has another crack in his face.

Lisa goes downstairs in the morning to find her father making pancakes. They are always thin and chewy and bland, but they are her favourite breakfast because sometimes when he is watching them cook and waiting to flip one, her father hums to himself. She likes the soft, tuneless little sound very much.

"Can you get the newspaper please, dear?" her mother asks. She doesn't really need to ask—Lisa gets the paper every day, just as her father reads it every day. Her father with his paper is a bit like his humming over pancakes.

"Quickly," her father says. "Breakfast is nearly ready."

When he looks at her she sees more cracks in his face. A small piece has broken away, leaving a pale grey divot of rock exposed below one eye.

He is not going to make it through the day.

She runs out of the door, pretending she is hurrying because he has asked her to. The sky is clear and blue and very unfair.

"Good morning, Lisa."

The voice is too cheerful, just like the day is too pleasant.

Gerry is short, and thin, and has dark hair that flops into his eyes. He is grinning on the other side of the low fence between the houses—he is always grinning, or frowning, or yelling. He is younger than Lisa, but already has deep wear marks on either side of his mouth. She can see the white, chalky limestone there, and in the deep crease between his eyes.

"Hello, Gerry," Lisa says, and picks up the paper.

"What's wrong?" he asks. She does not know how he can tell. His grin is gone, his frown sudden and deep. It is unnerving, the changes he goes through.

It is breathtaking.

"My father is cracking," she says. Her voice is steady, as it should be.

"My parents have some cracks," Gerry says. He doesn't understand.

"Granite is hard," Lisa tells him, "but brittle. We can last a long time, but we have to be careful."

He still looks confused.

"Granite does not wear down easily," she says. "When we start to break, it does not stop."

And then he gets it. He frowns, and there is deep sympathy in his eyes now. It is so dizzying, everything he is being right there on his face.

"I'm so sorry, Lisa," he says.

"It is how we are." She wants to say more, but does not. It's always strange, talking to this soft limestone boy.

The Andersons let everything out. They wear so quickly. Lisa does not understand it.

"Well, I'm really sorry," he says, and reaches across the small fence and touches her arm. "Let me know if you need to talk."

By mid-afternoon Lisa's father has lost one eye, and what remains of his face is a spiderweb of cracks and broken pieces. When she takes him a cup of coffee in the sunroom, he has to use his left hand as his right has crumbled away, leaving only small pieces on the floor.

"Thank you," he says, his voice still clear. Lisa tells him he is welcome, and he nods.

"Tell your mother it is nearly time, please. I cannot hold it all in much longer."

Lisa walks quickly from the room.

Her mother is in the laundry room again—just standing there, staring at a pile of folded shirts. They are flannelette work shirts, the ones Lisa's father wears when he rakes leaves and clears the gutters.

Her mother's face is smooth, as unmarked as always.

"Yes, dear?"

"Father says it will be soon."

Her mother runs both hands down the front of her dress. It is a nice dress. The one with orange flowers that her father bought her.

"Very well," her mother says. "Shall we go?"

Lisa knows she should say yes. They are granite, after all.

Instead, she shakes her head.

"You don't have much time," her mother says, and then goes past her daughter out of the laundry.

Lisa doesn't go looking for Gerry—he is just a limestone boy, and soft. It is only a coincidence that she walks out and stands in the front yard, near the fence, near where they talked earlier. And it must be a coincidence that he is just there, sitting on the front porch of his house. He comes down to the fence.

"Did...did it happen?" he asks. She can hear so much in his voice. It is all right there, right on top.

She shakes her head. She could speak, but she doesn't want to hear her own bland response, not straight after his voice.

"I don't understand," he says, as if she had asked, "how you can keep so much in?"

She does not understand how he can let so much out. Lisa has seen Gerry's parents plenty of times. Their weathered faces are a map of white, chalky creases from tears and frowns and smiles. Their smile marks are especially deep, worn into the soft rock of their being as if their pleasure were running water. Once, Lisa saw Gerry's mother laugh so hard that chalky dust floated down like fine mist.

"You wear away so quickly," she says, and Gerry's sudden smile is bemused.

"Do we?" he asks. "It doesn't seem like it."

She is back in the sunroom in time. Of course she is.

Her mother sits on the arm of her father's chair. They are holding hands. His only has two fingers left.

He looks at Lisa with his one eye. More of his face is cracked and broken grey stone now, but his mouth is still mostly there.

"Are you both ready?" he asks, like it is something happening to them. Which it is, Lisa knows. She is not ready, but she is granite. She nods.

"Yes, dear," her mother says.

Her father draws a deep breath. And smiles.

"I could not have wished for a better life than with both of you," he says. There is a breaking sound as part of his body slumps inwards.

"You have made everything worth it," he says, and a long piece of grey stone falls from his already broken face.

"I love you both very much."

His smile widens, and a tear runs from his one eye. And then he is gone, breaking apart into small pieces of grey stone, pieces flecked with minerals that shine in the afternoon sun.

Lisa sits with her mother, and tries not to break herself.

Granite is hard, but it is so very brittle.

"It happened," she says to Gerry as she sits on the front steps, but she does not look up. He was there when she came outside.

Maybe he had just come outside again himself. Maybe he had been waiting.

He says nothing.

"I might break," she says finally. Her voice is conversational.

She is surprised that she did not crack, split right down the middle, sitting there in the sunroom. She had thought her mother might, maybe just sob and crumble right there next to her husband, but when Lisa had looked at her, her mother just nodded.

"I'm not going anywhere," she said.

That had been all, but it had almost been too much. It might still be too much.

Now, she looks at Gerry. He already has two soft tracks of white where his tears usually run down his face, and there are fresh, wet lines there now.

"Don't cry," she says. "You will wear yourself down."

"Can't you cry?" he asks. There is no accusation in his voice. Not even curiosity. It is more like a plea. Like he still has hope she can be something else.

"No," Lisa says, "I have to be careful, if I want to last."

They sit together. Lisa does not shed any tears. She holds herself tightly. She keeps it all in.

"I'm so sorry," Gerry says.

She does not reply. She watches him cry, and wonders how long it will be before she breaks.

Fermi's Paradox Box

Dr Henty knocked on the door and went in without waiting. He might stand outside all day waiting for Professor Clarke to realise someone was there, otherwise.

Katie Clarke looked up, her eyes watery and tired, as Henty planted himself in front of her desk. She blinked and pushed her glasses up her nose. He tried not to smile, and failed.

"Yes?" she said, frowning like this large smiling man was a troublesome proof that needed solving.

"Katie, you need to go home. It's way past five," Henty said. He should be more forceful than that, but he just couldn't. He was supposed to be in charge, make sure those like Clarke didn't get too bogged down in work, that they didn't burn out. But she did love it so.

"I think I'm on to something," Clarke said. Her hair was perhaps a bit more uncontrolled than usual, her desk a mess of papers and notes. But she was smiling as she gestured at the high-end laptop that was humming far too loudly. It would be simulating something beyond its capacity, no doubt. This rather distracted polymath of a woman had already burnt out three computers in four weeks.

"Katie, you solved the timeline issue of the Fermi Paradox. You've shown the probabilities of contact with an alien race are almost at certainty. Remember? You'll most likely be nominated for the Nobel."

Henty didn't like how plaintive he was sounding. He cleared his throat before continuing. "Maybe it's time to have a break. Do a bit of self-care."

"What? No! I mean, I'm really on to something," she replied, like he hadn't heard that part.

Clarke turned her computer around to reveal a screen of rapidly scrolling numbers, sequence after sequence, moving far too quickly for him to actually read.

"You know I'm a sociologist as well as other stuff," she said. "My Fermi calculations were just the start."

She snatched up a piece of paper covered in scribble and waved it above her head like a flag.

"Factor in Darwinian-based biological imperatives and our long history of societal, um, clashes, and the outcome of contact has an eighty-eight percent chance of being detrimental!"

"Detrimental?" Henty repeated slowly. "How, exactly?"

Clarke brought down her piece of paper and regarded it with some consternation.

"I don't know," she said. "But it will be something terrible, no doubt."

Superintendent Gordux made sure the door behind him was locked before he pulled his Henty face off. He sighed with relief as he stretched his mandibles out.

"If we are so advanced, why can't we make a species mask that is comfortable?" he asked. Yes, he was irritated, but not really by the mask.

Batzultax glanced up from the panel of displays and waved his front limb at the image of Clarke in her office.

"Why did you suggest she slow down?" the technician asked. "Bit pointless now, isn't it? She has already solved the probability of contact approaching certainty. What do they call it? The Fermi Paradox?" He made a rude gesture with his mandibles. "Like some human physicist was the first to ever have the thought."

"The woman still needs a break," Gordux said.

"She won't take one," Batzultax replied. "Even with our early checks of her she got her solution of their so-called Fermi Paradox almost too quickly," Batzultax continued. "We scooped her up barely in time, and wiping us from her thoughts didn't slow her down at all. She really powered on through."

Gordux scratched at his mandibles. He shouldn't, he knew. It was bad manners. But Batzultax was still eyeing the displays.

"Maybe her simulated habitat matches her real life too closely," Gordux said, tapping one scaled cheek in thought. "All she does is work. We should've given her some distractions. A love interest? Something like that."

"I don't know why you are bothering," Batzultax said. "She is basically done and she stuffed it up, just like we thought humans would."

He tapped a claw on the screen showing Clarke at work. "The system states it is pretty much a certainty she will attack you once she works out exactly what you are," Batzultax sighed. "She's bright, but humans, they just aren't ready. She shouldn't be basing her calculations on their own history, for a start. Detrimental contact! As if we are all like them." He clacked his own mandibles in disgust. "You know what needs to happen. I just need your order."

Batzultax was looking at him now, but Gordux scratched his mandible anyway.

"Katie is not the whole human race," he said. He shouldn't, but he couldn't help it. Gordux didn't know what the difference really was between humans and them, given what was supposed to happen next. He managed not to say that, though. There was no point in trying to argue.

"You have to follow procedure," Batzultax said.

"She looks so happy, scribbling away in there," Gordux replied. "Let's give her another day or so before we, ah, terminate her tenure."

Professor Clarke always caught the number 42 bus from her small apartment near the University campus, and got off one stop short to get her large soy latte at the Fried Pickle Café. Always. It made the simulation of her surrounding environment quite efficient, even if Gordux sometimes found himself wishing she would do something else. Branch out. Try a different caffeinated beverage, even. Something less predictable.

She also always came to work early, and since his species had a similar sleep pattern to hers, Gordux knew he could intercept her at the café before Batzultax took up his own work post.

"Oh, hello!" Clarke said on her way out as Henty appeared, blocking the doorway.

"Dr Clarke," he said. "Katie. I need to talk to you, and it needs to be right now."

Katie stopped with her drink halfway to her mouth.

"Perhaps we should wait until work, Dr Henty," she said, slightly wary.

Damn. He had put her off guard, and there was no time. If he was going to break the rules, he should just go ahead and break them.

He reached up and pulled off his mask. He stretched his mandibles out, like she wouldn't notice them if he didn't. Professor Clarke very slowly lowered her soy latte. Her eyes went very large. Gordux had not known human eyes could get that large.

No one else in the café missed a beat, which made sense. The system had not been programmed to react to Gordux's real visage.

"Katie, don't be afraid," he said quickly. "But I need to get you out of here. I need to... well, I need to give you another chance."

He still had no idea what he was doing. This went against everything he was supposed to do. The procedures were in place for very, very good reasons.

But it wasn't right. Clarke was predicting detrimental contact, and they were going to make her prediction correct, at least for her.

Besides, he liked Katie.

Suddenly, everything froze. A woman in the corner had her head tilted back, her mouth open in silent laughter. The barista was pouring milk, the long thread of white liquid connecting the jug to the cup static, not flowing. The cars going by outside stopped, like someone had barked a command at them. Everything was on pause.

Except Katie. She smiled, and then reached up and pulled off her own face.

"Finally!" she said, and scratched at a mandible. "You took your time!"

"What...what is going on?" Gordux stammered, staring at the not-so-Professor Clarke, and then around at the frozen scene of the café.

"You *are* in a simulation, Gordux, but it has been for your benefit, not mine. We need to vet our applicants thoroughly."

"Vet? But I'm on a mission. And I was going to vaporise you," Gordux said.

"No, you aren't on a mission yet, and no, you apparently weren't going to vaporise me."

"I don't understand," Gordux said, because that was all he was currently sure of.

Katie nodded and scratched at one of her mandibles again. "We will give you your full memory back shortly. But it is time to give Earth an answer to their Fermi Paradox."

"But everyone is sure they aren't ready," Gordux said.

"You didn't seem so sure," Katie replied.

"I said Professor Clarke was not the whole human race," Gordux replied. "Which was apparently truer than I realised."

"Well," Katie replied, "you gave her a second chance. If the human race reacts badly to your presence, you can decide if they get one as well."

She held up a finger.

"If you think they deserve one."

Maintenance

The Bot is all long limbs and careful movements, a model designed for small tasks and companionship. Every time it moves its joints grind very softly.

"Don't you have a maintenance routine?" Hubert asks as he holds up the abstract bookend, a thing of stylised swirls and loops. One of his mother's friends will think it is the perfect keepsake, no doubt.

"Yes," the Bot replies.

It pulls a dark blouse with dusty sequins from the cupboard. Hubert can practically smell the mothballs from across the room. The Bot holds the piece of clothing for a long time without moving.

"That can go in the donations," Hubert says. It is pointless getting the Bot to do something like this. The robot's central AI is supposed to adapt to a user's needs, but the thing had been with his mother for so long it probably can't adjust to what he wants. Clear the place out and go, that is the plan. He needs to remember that.

The robot bends to add the blouse to the pile of shoes and coats and other things an older woman accrues over a lifetime. Hubert looks away, trying not to recall that blouse. Those red shoes. His mother, younger, vibrant, smiling down at him.

Spin, Huey! Spin with me, Huey!

So many times. How he had laughed as she spun, her arms outflung. How she had laughed when he tried. A lifetime ago. Beyond a barrier of hard words, foolish words.

The robot moves with that soft, grinding noise.

"Can you do your maintenance, then? You sound like you need it."

"Yes," the Bot says as it picks up a vase with a dried flower in it in one hand and a faded Broadway poster in the other.

"I don't know what those are," Hubert says. "Put them in the junk pile."

The Bot does not put the flower or the poster in the discard pile.

"Some of these things were valuable to your mother," the Bot says.

"Well, she was wrong!" Hubert snaps. He snatches the poster from the robot and drops it with the other pieces of his mother's life he knows nothing of. "None of this stuff matters."

An old dance poster. A dried flower, maybe from years ago. She must have left more. Must have cared.

The robot stands as still as only a robot can, holding its dead flower. Hubert tries to speak again. His throat is tight.

"Did she say anything?" he bursts out finally. "About me?"

"You have not visited in three years and two months."

Hubert clenches his fists. "I know that! Tell me something she said!"

He wonders if he is about to hit the robot. That would be pointless. As pointless as talking to the thing. As pointless as being here now, too late. He forces his hands to relax. He doesn't know what he wants. Except that is not true. He wants it to be like it was. He wants what he can't have. He wants her smiling down at him, the years gone. The distance gone.

Yay! Spin, Huey!

"General conversation is bound by confidentiality," the Bot says. "Perhaps she left a message during one of the calls she attempted to you."

No, she hadn't. Mostly hang ups. Sometimes that deep silence full of ache and sorrow. Once, an indrawn breath like she was about to speak. She could have told him she was sick. Or he could have answered, even just once.

He could have called.

It hurts. Could have. Should have. But didn't.

"Get out of here," he tells the Bot. "Go and do your maintenance routine before you seize up completely."

The robot is just standing in the yard.

"That can't be part of your maintenance," Hubert says from the doorway.

"No," the robot says. "My standard routine is a series of movements designed to rotate and lubricate my joints and expel particles. It increases longevity by a factor of three."

"Did my mother leave a letter for me? Did she write something down?"

"Not that I am aware of," the Bot says.

"Maybe she didn't have time," Hubert says.

"That is possible," the Bot says. "While she knew she was ill for some months, the end was sudden."

That's not something Hubert wants to dwell on. "Well, get on with it, then," he says. "We've got work to do."

“My routine has been altered,” the Bot says. “It requires supervision.”

“That sounds like a waste of time,” Hubert says.

“I need to confirm you will supervise, Hubert,” the Bot says.

“Fine,” Hubert says.

Perhaps his mother left something written for him that the robot is unaware of. He should check her bedside cabinet again.

The Bot sets its arms at shoulder height. Hubert watches absently, biting his lip. Maybe she had given up reaching out. He had not answered so many calls.

The robot turns, one metal heel digging into the grass. Its arms are still outstretched at shoulder height.

It spins around once. Then again. Faster, but not too fast. Arms outstretched. No—outflung. It spins again, and Hubert stares.

The Bot turns, and Hubert moves slowly down the steps. The robot spins in its altered routine. It spins its message out, across more distance than the yard, across the years. Beyond the barriers of harsh words and unanswered calls. Hubert knows what he is going to hear before the words are spoken.

“Spin, Huey!” the robot calls out. “Spin with me, Huey!”

Planting his heel in the grass, Hubert raises his own arms. Crying, he begins to spin.

The Complete and Utter Drag of Becoming the Self-Taught Ghost Poet of Mars

I am the Ghost of Mars. Self-titled, but who else is doing the naming? And it's not like I've got much else to do. How many times can you watch the sun come up through a smear of dirty sky before you want to scream, or cry, or maybe just go crazy? What a joke the afterlife is.

"Don't you want more?"

That was what my best friend Leo used to ask me.

In school he could really psych you up with talk of what we'd do after. Where we would go. He'd get this look in his eyes and he stare off past my shoulder like he was seeing grand vistas and crowded streets of distant cities and all that shit. After school, though, he wouldn't quit it. Not even after we landed our factory jobs, one suburb over from where we grew up. It was like he didn't notice all the faces around us *were* us, just a bit more worn out. He was always going on about getting out, getting more, getting...something. It got too hard to listen to his drivel.

"Leave it be!" I snapped at him that day. It was so goddam hot, and I was supposed to be over on Floor B, helping with the scrap iron. Even hotter over there, and I hated the heat. Funny how I miss even that, now that I can't feel anything. Funny, but not, you know, *ha ha* funny.

"Grunts like us don't go anywhere," I spat. "So why don't you shut up about it?"

I turned away and stomped down the walkway, ignoring the hurt look on his face. Harsh, and I wouldn't have said it if I knew they were going to be my last words, but whoever gets the privilege of knowing that? Besides, it was supposed to be true. I wasn't supposed to go anywhere.

I wish I hadn't.

I don't know if there are a lot of ghosts. I don't know if it just happens to some people. Maybe if you were a sailor centuries ago and you plummeted to your death from the crow's nest and splattered on the planks, then you were a ship ghost. And then the ship wore out, and they pried up the boards and turned them into a—god, I don't know, a bespoke side cabinet for some New England manor house—then you became a house ghost, haunting a pastel bedroom, hanging around through the years until the owners turned the place into a Bed and Breakfast and you had to watch sad, middle-age couples screw and pretend they weren't trying to hide away from their three kids and their mortgage for a couple of days.

I can say with absolute certainty what happens when you stomp away from your best friend on a factory walkway that collapses, and you bleed out on a roll of wiring that eventually gets cleaned up and shipped out to another factory that makes electronics. Then, guess what? Factory ghost. Then NASA lab ghost, desert testing-ground ghost, launch ghost. Space ghost for a bit, which is not as cool as it sounds. Not much to do in space.

I guess here at least I get to watch dust blow about.

And pout.

Huh. That rhymes.

I can move a couple of hundred yards from the Rover. If I go too far it's like I'm on the end of a rubber band. I can push it a few more steps, but not much. Add that to the hundred or so yards the Rover can move in a day, and man, I really get about. A few more months and we might even get over the first little hill, get a look around. Maybe the dust is a different shade of red over there.

I used to think the months when the Rover was being tested sucked. Out in the shitty desert, watching again and again as the little metal handcart was put through its paces. I thought I hated that place. I thought it was boring. What did I know?

There was one thing, though, that made it cool. Well, a person, not a thing.

Dhama.

"You're so lucky," she would say sometimes. She was one of the engineers. She would stare right through me at the Rover's insides with her deep, dark eyes, and this little half smile would play on her face as she poked at the electronics. She was the only one who spoke to the Rover, and she did it no matter who was around. One time one of the grey-haired, dried-up old egg-heads said something to her about it and she told him where to stick his laptop. So she was either really important, or a spunk, or mental. Or all three.

"You will be the first to actually be there," she would say, as she fiddled with the Rover's antennae, or ran diagnostics, or whatever. "You will see the sun rise through that red dust before any of us."

There was a note in her voice when she spoke to the Rover that reminded me of Leo. Wistful. Wanting. It made me want to tell her...something. Maybe that she should do whatever she wanted to do before it was too late. That late came earlier than you thought. But guess what? I've never been good at talking to girls, and death had not improved the situation.

Sunrise, sunset, once again? You bet. Maybe I can be a poet. The Ghost Poet of Mars, busting my rhymes out to the great empty. I suck, but I might get better. I've lost track of time, or it has lost track of me. It's all just red dirt, red dust, red sky. I don't even get to feel the sting of the grit in my eyes.

I do like night time, though. The stars never seem to be the same.

Twinkle, twinkle
Little stars,
Guess who's stuck,
Stuck on Mars?

Around and around we go, where we stop, of course I know. We are doing a damn loop in this crater. I'll never get to see what is over that hill. Every time the Rover stops its incessant crawl, I can hear whirring and other soft noises from inside. It certainly thinks it's busy doing important work. Why didn't I pay attention out in the desert instead of mooning over Dhama? I might know why the damn thing is going in circles. Not that it would help.

Why didn't I pay attention when Mrs Vickery was going on about poems in English?

There once was a ghost in a crater
Of education he was always a hater
No focus in school
After death stays the fool
Now poetry he hopes will come later.

Months? Years? How long is either on Mars? How long do ghosts last? I mean, I never saw any others in my oh-so-extensive travels from factory to shiny white lab to desert. No other translucent, sad-faced spectres floating around launch command. Surely NASA had a few skeletons in their closet? Am I an anomaly? Am I real? Maybe I'm in hell. What rhymes with hell? Yell? Smell? Or are they just things I can't do? Words are all I have left, so why don't I know more of them? I can't just do limericks forever. And what good are poems if you have no one to tell them to?

My life is red dust

Forever silence and void
I ache for colours.
What did Vickery call that? A high something.

The Rover has stopped moving. It has a pretty thick layer of fine red dirt on it now. I think I've been here for a long time.

Last night after the dust dropped, I saw what I thought I'd seen the night before. A light in the sky. I mean, there are so many—when it's not dusty, it's so clear the stars are like white shards of ice, cold and deathly and beautiful. It takes my breath away (ha ha). But this one was zooming along in a straight line. An orbit? Not like I would know. It looks bigger tonight, though.

Stars through dust,
Out of reach. Frozen. Timeless.
Her dark eyes see through me
I fade.
I persist.

The lander comes down just as the sun comes up. I mean, I guess it's a lander? It doesn't look the size of a rocket or anything.

I doubt it's going to do much landing, though. Expensive high-tech gear isn't supposed to spin as much as that as it falls. It also shouldn't be trailing a half-open parachute.

What a mess this is going to be.

When the Rover landed I imagined all the cheers and clapping and hugging back on Earth, the sort of thing you would see on the news.

I don't want to imagine what the response is to this.

The lander hits the ground completely upside down, its rounded nose cone smashing into the red surface so hard that dust and rocks go everywhere. There is an explosion and a gout of flame, but not as much as you would expect from a movie or anything. Still, at least one very large piece of metal goes flying straight through me. There is an ugly tearing sound, and I turn to see the Rover is now two half-Rovers, sheared clean through the middle.

I'm not that sad about it, to be honest.

"Hello?"

I turn back to the burning lander, and she is standing right there next to it. She is in a suit, a spacesuit, but she has no helmet on. Her dark eyes are wide, and behind her I can see a hand sticking out from the wreckage. It's her hand, limp and bloody.

I know her. I'd laugh, not believe it could be her, could not be Dhama of the dark eyes, but she had wanted this so much. Well, not this exactly.

"The ship—it malfunctioned. I was the only one who made it to the lander," she says. She stares at me, and then all around. "What happened? Who are you?"

I can't tell her she's dead. Not straight away. But I'm going to say something, damn it. I open my mouth with no idea of what is going to come out.

"Do you like poetry?" I ask.

Location, Velocity, End Point

Three more days of going over my calculations, of checking and rechecking, of trying to think and not think at the same time. It cannot work, and yet it has to work. There are too many variables, an infinity of possible outcomes. I need just one.

I input the final sequence and sit, my hands hovering over the controls. Heisenberg was more right than he knew. I know exactly where I am, God help me. It makes it almost impossible to go in the right direction, at the right velocity. Practically impossible to find the end point I am searching for. But if I can get it right this time, just one time, maybe I can fix the only thing that really matters.

I submit my calculations.

The light on the capsule door flickers from red to green and the lock disengages. The door swings open and this time, *this time*, it is not an alien, implacable sky, or the lush, tropical nightmare of the distant past. It is my kitchen—blue sky outside the window, white tiles on the floor. There is the soft hum of the refrigerator, and the smell of lemon detergent. My heart trips and stumbles over its own surging hope. I see him.

"Tommy!" I shout. My boy looks up from his trains. His curly locks fall into his big blue eyes, and he smiles, a pure, joyful smile. I feel my own rising to match it. But then he falters, and his eyelids flutter, and he slumps down into an untidy heap. My smile freezes, turns to a scream. Of all the times, of all the possibilities—I wish it had been another ancient ruin, a molten planet, foreign skies that twisted and churned, some unknown reality at the end of my untrustworthy calculations. Anything other than this.

I have lived this moment before. It is etched in too-bright colours in my mind, how I found him on the white tiles, six months after his own terminal trajectory could have been altered. Next will come the ambulance, the hospital, the prognosis. Heisenberg would be proud. I know exactly where I am. I am too late.

The capsule is a tangle of wires and circuit boards and pieces of paper with scrawled calculations. At first I thought it would be easy. A window of time, a toddler's span of a target, a triplet of years in which to warn of the creeping illness within. But now all I see are my desperate attempts to limit infinity with indefinite integrals, my inability to catch such a minuscule span of history in a prison of Hessian matrices. Location, velocity. End point. There are too many variables.

I push aside a nest of copper wire and insulation and dig down with a shaking hand. He is there, just as he is not. A round faced little boy, my little man, looking out solemnly from behind the glass frame. He stares across the gulf between unsolvable equations. I have succeeded. I have failed. I circle the point I need, a window of time and location that lies hidden like a treasured image buried under nonsense. I have gotten close. I have missed wildly. Certainty grows at the expense of hope. I turn back to the console, and fling myself backwards, outwards, onwards.

"Play trains, Daddy?"

I had not realised he was awake. I sit by the bed, staring at nothing. I am so tired, but the notepad is filled despite my weariness, filled with numbers that mean nothing, numbers that I had wished meant everything. Tommy's voice is low, almost a whisper. He holds a bright red train out to me, his hand trembling.

"Yes," I say. My voice is also a whisper. I take the red train and finally look at him. He is so pale, and so drawn, his eyes too large, too bright. He smiles at me. He smiles for me.

"Sick," he says.

"Yes," I reply, my voice so low I'm sure he can't hear me. "I'm sorry."

He frowns. "Daddy. Smile, daddy."

I try to smile. I try not to crush the toy train in my hand. I know where I am with a certainty no theoretical physicist ever postulated. I know where I am, and I know where this is going. I am sure now, and my hope is dead on the page in front of me.

I look at my boy. He is frail, and failing. I know what failure looks like, and what frailty feels like. My notepad is full of both. I cannot know where I am and where I am going. I would trade so much for a drop of uncertainty in those numbers. I would trade everything. Uncertainty would mean hope.

It is a moment later, the moment before, and somewhere in between. I am in the capsule but I am also nowhere. Location, velocity. End point. I am unmoored between the lines of my own calculations. I input the reduced set of calculations, the smaller number of variables, the lack of my own point within infinity. There can be no return. This time, it must work, and yet I cannot be sure. I do not want to be sure. I wait once more, one final time, and after another lifetime compressed into a moment the light turns from red to green. The door opens, and I see blue sky beyond a window. I see white tiles. I step forward, full of uncertainty. And once more, full of hope.

Universes all the way Down

It looked like Toby's table. It looked like his little kitchen too, in his house, with his refrigerator over by the sink—but the dark, starry expanse of space outside the window wasn't the usual view. The tall, grey alien sitting opposite him was also new.

"Don't be alarmed," the alien said.

"Bit hard not to be," Toby replied. "Where have the rhododendrons gone?"

The alien looked a bit confused (although in all honesty it was a bit hard to tell). Toby gestured out of the window. "The garden," he said. And then, after a thought, "And the street. I guess the street is more important than the hedge. Although it is a nice hedge."

"You are not in your house," the alien said. "We are just trying to make you comfortable."

"Well, you aren't doing a great job of it," Toby said.

The alien blinked with more than the usual number of eyelids, and seemed to glance towards the fridge for a moment. The fridge said nothing.

"Look," the alien said. "We don't want you upset. We don't want you to think we've abducted you or anything. We don't go in for that sort of thing anymore."

"Seems a lot like being abducted."

"It's not!" the alien said, and looked to the fridge again. This time the fridge made an odd noise.

"And that doesn't help," Toby said, pointing at the fridge.

"We will take you back," the alien said. "You should feel honoured, you know. The last time we did this, the human became quite well known. Famous, as you humans say."

"But my rhododendrons are alright?"

"Humans have a lot of potential," it said, ignoring the question. "Every now and then you get the wrong end of things, as you say. Sometimes we help out."

"This hardly seems like helping out," Toby said, looking between the alien and the fridge. "Here, I only bought groceries yesterday. I hope you aren't stuffing around with the milk."

"This isn't your house!" the alien said again, a bit testily, then made an effort to calm itself.

"Given your background in physics, this shouldn't be too hard, and shouldn't take too long. Then we will take you back to your, ah, milk."

Toby frowned but said nothing.

"Well, we just wanted to let you humans know that, ah, the experimental conclusions in neutrino asymmetry are a bit, well, wrong."

"What?"

"You know, the experiment that has shown that flavours of neutrinos shift from what is expected." The alien paused, and when Toby said nothing, it huffed.

"The charge-conjugation and parity reversal violation?" it asked, its voice rising significantly.

"What are you talking about?" Toby said. "What has this got to do with my milk?"

"The study that was just published? That very nearly explains why there is more matter than antimatter in the universe?"

Toby shook his head.

The alien huffed and glanced at the fridge before ploughing on. "Well, it's wrong, you see. This universe is dominated by matter because it is leaking in from the universe underneath this one. That one is mostly antimatter, which keeps pushing matter up into this universe."

Toby looked between the alien and the fridge again. "Seems like you could've just made a phone call. You have phones, I suppose?"

The alien dropped its hands to the table. "Well, but there is more to it. Calculations and proofs and, well, that sort of thing. We thought we would show you before you went home."

Toby shook his head. "I wouldn't understand nothing like that. Now, my neighbour Dr. Stanislov, he might. Funny chap, with one of those continental-type accents, but he does physics. Nice enough, I suppose, although it's a bit hard to follow on with what he is saying sometimes. But he trims his side of the hedge every other week. Keeps it nice. Maybe you could write all this stuff down, and I could show it to him? He might be able to explain it."

The alien blinked its numerous eyelids rapidly and looked at the fridge. The fridge made a series of harsh-sounding noises that no fridge really has any right to make.

"How would I know how it happened?" the alien snapped. "I'm not in charge of targeting." It covered its face with its long-fingered hands for a moment and moaned softly. Then it dropped its hands. "We had better turn around."

The stars out of the window shifted. The alien stayed seated, but seemed to be avoiding looking at both him and the fridge. Toby fidgeted. The silence grew longer, until he had a thought.

"Here," he said. "But if this stuff, this matter, is leaking in from underneath, being pushed up, then what's happening in that other place?"

"What?" The alien said. "What do you mean? The antimatter universe?"

Toby nodded. "So does that mean that other stuff, the antimatter, is leaking into that universe?"

The alien nodded thoughtfully. "Yes, I suppose it must."

"Then what about the next universe below that one? Is it leaking?"

The alien opened its mouth, and then closed it slowly. It glanced at the fridge, which did nothing.

"It must be," it said finally, and blinked.

"Then where's the start? I mean, where did the leak start?"

"I don't know," the alien said.

Toby suddenly felt bad. Maybe he shouldn't be asking questions about such complicated things. It was just that he liked things to be neat and tidy, like his hedge. Perhaps he could ask Dr. Stanislov when he got home. He seemed quite bright, really.

"Look, don't worry about it," Toby finally said, still feeling a bit rotten. "Maybe it's just universes all the way down."

Optimal Care

"Hey, T! You about?"

James rounds the corner of the kitchen, his dark hair lank, his face pale, his breathing all-too-shallow.

Tenderbot is standing at the kitchen island bench. It pushes the sandwich and milk forward. The Home Care Unit has already scanned the boy and computed a 92% chance he will reject the sandwich, but Tenderbot always attempts to optimise care.

James sits down and opts for the glass.

"Your platelet count is down. Eat," Tenderbot says.

"Oh, come on, T. You think a sandwich is going to save me?"

"A sandwich will not save you, James."

The boy grins and wipes at his milk moustache.

"We've got to get you that upgrade, T," he says. "If only so you can know how funny you are."

Tenderbot says nothing. A response is not required.

James sips his milk and grins wider.

"I'm just yanking your chain. Here, look at this."

He unfolds a piece of paper and slides it across the benchtop. Tenderbot notes the slight tremble of the boy's hands.

"An actual real flier!" James exclaims. "Can you believe it? They're stuck up all over school. Talk about retro."

Tenderbot picks up the flimsy thing. The static display is multi-coloured, and obviously human designed. The proportions are very incorrect. There are fireworks, but the trajectories do not align properly, and the blast patterns are far from reasonable. The banner headline is in various unnecessary colours. All of it is very poorly executed. Entirely suboptimal.

"You Can Dance If You Want To. You Can Leave Your Cares Behind!" Tenderbot reads the headline out loud and scans the date and other details. "This is a social event."

"Yeah, and it's not far away," James replies. "I might even make it."

"The distance is not far. You could certainly attend."

James's grin fades a little.

"You sure are funny, T."

Tenderbot is 87% sure this is incorrect.

Tenderbot is wrapping the sandwich and cleaning the kitchen while James is talking to his father. Tenderbot monitors the stress levels in the father's voice, detects the disappointment in the son's. Finally, James logs off.

"He can't get back until the end of the month."

"The expense your father incurred purchasing me means—"

"I know, T. Expense all round. Who knew dying would suck the life out of two people?"

This is 100% incorrect. "Your father is stressed but his health has been satisfactory."

Just then the Holo beeps. James glances at the caller ID and his pale face goes white.

"Shit. Shit!" He stares at the screen.

"I will decline the call," Tenderbot says, reaching out.

"No!" James says, and hits the answer button.

The face projected above the screen is so red Tenderbot begins to move forward to adjust the contrast. Then the bot registers the dilated pupils and the way the girl touches her own lips lightly with two trembling fingers. The colouring problem is emotional, then, and adjusting the contrast will be of limited assistance.

"Um, hi, Jackie," James says.

"Hi," the girl replies.

"Hi," James says again.

There is silence. Tenderbot leans forward. "That is a suboptimal response. And your heart rate has increased. Are you in distress?"

"Shit, T!" James says, his face flashing from too white to a crimson that almost matches his caller.

The girl's eyes widen. "Is that a Home Care Unit?"

James manages a shaky little laugh. "Yeah. A Tenderbot. Would you mind not telling anyone? I get enough sad eyes at school already."

"Wow. Your family must be loaded." The girl stops, and her red face goes even redder. She puts one hand over her eyes. "Oh, I'm sorry. I didn't mean—I didn't think—"

James laughs again, louder this time. Tenderbot watches their halting conversation a moment longer. It appears suboptimal, but this time Tenderbot is only 63% certain.

Tenderbot is administering James's nightly treatment, adjusting the dosage carefully based on the day's antibody levels and the rate of cell metastasis, when the boy speaks.

"Hey, T," he says, a little dreamily. The meds have that effect. By morning the boy will be eager and energised, but perhaps a little less so than the day before. Soon there will come a time when these drugs will do more harm than good.

"Yes?"

"I need a favour," James says.

"If it is within my operational parameters, of course," Tenderbot says.

The boy's smile widens even as his eyes close.

"I need you to teach me how to dance."

Tenderbot does not reply. The boy has fallen asleep.

"Hey, T, you about?"

James enters the kitchen. Today he is steady on his feet, but slow. Tenderbot pushes the plate across the bench. There are two sandwiches. The Home Care Unit has calculated a 9% chance James will eat even one of the sandwiches, but that should increase significantly in a moment.

"What's this?" James asks.

"It is two sandwiches," Tenderbot replies, and James rolls his eyes.

"Moderate exertion may assist with blood flow and mobility. I have accessed extensive online footage," Tenderbot continues. "You will not be able to undertake the more rigorous routines, but some of the movements that accompany slower music should be achievable and beneficial." Tenderbot indicates the plate. "If you are appropriately sustained."

"Are you blackmailing me?"

"I am optimising your care. I will not teach you to dance if it compromises your condition."

James rolls his eyes but picks up the first sandwich. Tenderbot has indeed optimised the interaction.

In addition to numerous dance tutorials, Tenderbot has reviewed several films of the approximate era the social event aligns with.

"The slow dance is the pivotal point of the social event. It is also the only dance you may physically be capable of performing," it tells James.

"Thanks for the vote of confidence," the boy replies.

"You must place one hand around my waist, and also hold this hand," Tenderbot continues, and steps close to the boy.

"This is a bit weird," James says, but places his hand in Tenderbot's.

An old style power ballad emanates softly from the Care Unit's mouth.

"So weird," James mutters.

"This is not a waltz, although there appear to be movements in common," Tenderbot says. The music continues to come from its mouth as it speaks.

"According to the footage, the key is to stay close, and align footfalls without hindering your partner. Who leads may be a discussion point for you and your partner, but I will do so now."

Tenderbot steps to the side, and attempts to move James. James stumbles and steps on Tenderbot's foot.

"That is to be expected," Tenderbot states. "Practice will optimise your performance."

Practice does not optimise James's performance.

"How can this be so hard?" James says. He is sitting on the couch. Tenderbot has insisted on a break. The boy's strength is flagging badly. "It's so easy in virtual."

"It is little more than repetitive swaying. But you do not appear to have the required coordination skills. Rhythm is the most commonly used term for what you lack."

"You don't do encouragement well, do you?" the boy replies.

"I recommend ceasing these practices, James," Tenderbot says. "Your condition is worsening."

"My condition is not going to do anything but worsen." James gasps just a little as he speaks.

"Overexertion may exacerbate your condition. There is currently only a 28% probability this will have a satisfactory outcome for you."

"T, I don't think you know what the hell you're talking about," James says. The words are confrontational, but the boy smiles a little, like the robot has said something funny.

But Tenderbot knows how low 28% is.

Tenderbot stands outside the door and listens to the Holo-call. Its interactions with James have definitely become suboptimal.

"Your bot doesn't want you to go to the dance?"

That is the girl, Jackie. Tenderbot is a Home Care Unit, tuned to detect changes in breathing, small gasps of effort, the sound of a fall in a distant part of a house. It can easily detect the distress in her voice from where it stands in the hallway.

"It changed its mind," James says.

"Are you getting...sicker?" she asks.

"No, no," James replies, which is not the truth. "T always goes on about optimising care," he adds quickly. "I think it's worried about stuffing up." That is closer to the truth.

"Well, God forbid you should do something that isn't optimal." The girl puts enough emphasis on the last word that Tenderbot can tell she is trying to find humour in the situation, but James does not laugh.

The lessons have stopped. James has not complained.

The boy sits in the kitchen, his face pale, his eyes sunken and dark.

"What do you think we are left with, when it's all over?" James asks. "What is all the effort worth?"

Tenderbot can only answer in terms of itself: "I seek optimal task performance."

"And who will say your performance was optimal?" James's voice is low.

"I calculate that myself."

"So only you decide how you did."

"That is how I am programmed," Tenderbot confirms.

"T," James says, very softly, "I don't feel..."

The words fade to a whisper, and then James is toppling sideways. There is no danger of him falling, as Tenderbot has already registered the sudden drop in blood pressure and the fluttering eyelids as well as several other micro-indicators, and has caught the boy. It undertakes a full assessment as it carries James upstairs. As it does, it initiates a call to the boy's father, and another to the doctor.

The afternoon routine has changed. All routines have changed. Now it is treatments and bedrest and drug-induced sleep. Now it is waiting. Waiting for the treatments to lose effectiveness. Waiting for the boy's father to return. Tenderbot calculates the probability of recovery, or even partial recovery, again and again.

Tenderbot does not make sandwiches or try to get the boy to eat. James is mostly silent.

"The drugs that helped you through your daily activities are too strong for your body now, and must be halted," Tenderbot says.

"In light of your condition, both your father and your doctor have made it very clear you are not to attend this social event. The drugs required to sustain you for the event will reduce your subsequent quality of life substantially."

"I'm dying in bed. Let's not talk about quality of life," James says. He does not sound angry. Just tired.

"If you wish to be intimate with the girl Jackie, I can request of your father that she visit you here."

"No, T," James says. His pale cheeks flush with two small spots of pink, but he smiles slightly at the Home Care Unit.

"James, I do not understand why this event was so important. You can still participate in any one of numerous virtual activities."

James looks at the bot for a long time. The whites of his eyes are bloodshot, and his lips are dry, no matter how often Tenderbot applies salve.

"That would not be optimal," he says.

The '*Dance If You Want To!*' banner is too high on one side, or too low on the other. The stencilling is uneven. There are more poorly coloured depictions of fireworks. It is a very human display.

"T, can you let me walk in by myself?" James's face is pale, and he is already breathing too quickly. Tenderbot has administered the drugs that are necessary for the evening, and the boy will be able to walk unaided. There is a 79% chance it will be for the last time.

Jackie is standing at the entrance, underneath the suboptimal banner. Some of her peers laugh and jostle each other good-naturedly as they pass her by. Many are dressed in clothing reminiscent of the movie scenes Tenderbot has on file; amongst them, both stress levels and pleasure markers are running high.

Jackie sees Tenderbot and James and begins waving too vigorously.

As James waves back, Tenderbot releases its grip on the boy's arm. James starts away, but then stops and turns back.

"For what it's worth, T, I think your performance has been optimal," he says. "I'll see you soon, buddy."

James walks slowly to the girl and they go inside, arm in arm. Tenderbot looks at the crooked banner. It will assess its own performance, of course.

But not right now.

The Scythe and the Grey Witch

He weaves his way between the campfires and the huddled soldiers without looking at them. They are him, he is them, and none of them want to inspect each other too closely. There are a few low voices, but they are almost drowned out by the sound of blades being sharpened and the wind whipping the banners.

It is cold, and his chainmail is heavy. The mud sucks at his feet. The stumps of his two missing fingers ache, and the scar of the spear jab in his hip twinges. He does not care about those things at all.

He is trying not to care about anything.

His master's tent sits in the middle of the sprawling army. It's not a grand thing—just a slightly oversized, grey canvas shelter. There are no guards, but that says nothing. The Dark God's avatar does not spend much time there, and doesn't need guards anyway.

He pushes the flap aside and steps in without announcing himself. He is expected, and not even a half-sane person would enter this tent without being summoned. The inside is as hot as the night is cold, and for a moment his cheeks burn. There are torches that cast flickering light, and a brazier that burns with orange-green flames of unnatural heat.

The avatar, a dark and shapeless thing, sits slumped in its low chair.

The woman is sprawled in a circle of ash on the dirt floor in front of the avatar. Her grey dress is splattered with mud, and her long hair is dirty, hanging in clumps across her face. Her hands are tied with a thick, white rope. She doesn't look up or move. She had fought when they caught her, earlier in the day, but she had not been as troublesome as they expected. He had been there, as had the avatar.

"Ah," the avatar says in its voice of spitting fat and sizzling ice. "Jordan the Scythe. That is what you are called."

It's not a question, but Jordan answers anyway. "Yes, my Lord," he says. "That is what some of the other soldiers call me."

There is bubbling laughter as the inky shadow shifts. It has no arms, no legs, no head, but it stretches forward as if inspecting him.

"I hear they call you that because you are like the harvest. No lingering deaths. No fear on your part. Just reaping," it says. "I don't know if I like that."

It sits back, or seems to, and the laughter dies.

Jordan says nothing.

"The Dark God prefers the lingering," the blackness in the chair says.

Jordan bows his head. "My Lord, I do nothing but work towards fulfilling my pact in good faith."

"Good faith?" the avatar repeats, and there is that laughter again, dark and cold. "Oh, I do like that!"

Then it sobers again. "You are very close to the end of your service."

Jordan the Scythe knows. It is one of the things he has been carefully not thinking about. He is almost done. It is the only thing that matters, even now, even with the woman in the ash circle.

The avatar leans forward again, or seems to, the shadow of it stretching like it will spill from the chair.

"A soldierly task for you, Scythe. You did so well, you and the others, when we caught this one today. I am to go and report to my Lord. To our Lord."

Here one sliver of darkness moves out, a tendril, an arm, perhaps, pointing at the slumped woman. "We have wanted this one. The Grey Witch. He will want to know we have her. She is trapped in the circle, bound by the ash of the rowan tree, but she still needs guarding."

There is a pause, then. "You may stand watch outside, if you like." The avatar's voice is smooth and low and on the edge of laughter again.

Perhaps it knows. Perhaps it is enjoying this.

"Yes, my Lord," Jordan says. "Will I still attend the battle on the morrow?"

"Of course, of course," the creature, the splinter of the Dark God, says. "Tomorrow will be the final day of your service, yes?"

It does not wait to see if Jordan will reply. It draws back on the chair, keeps drawing in, pulling tight, tighter, closing in upon itself. The green-orange light flickers across the dark smear of it, the inky non-surface, and then there is nothing but the low chair.

Jordan, who turned his farmer's muscles to a warrior's scars and aches slowly and methodically, takes the avatar's chair to watch and wait for the morning. He regards the still form in the circle.

And he tries not to remember how much he loved her.

Jordan does not know how the other soldiers deal with their time in servitude. Some, he knows, sought out the Dark God eagerly, with little thought of pacts or tallies. They are the ones he avoids on the battleground, the ones that laugh, that foam, that shriek and gibber. Some others weep as they fight. Many of these are killed quickly, slashed and hammered down as they cry. Some just eventually slow, and then stop, their weapons drooping as the screams and blood and mud overwhelm them. They are worn down by their own actions moments before they are cut down.

The monsters and the weepers have the same thing in common. They think too much on what is happening, on what they have done. It is better to think of farming. To be the scythe, cutting the golden stalks, sweeping, sweeping, letting the day pass in a haze, letting time go, letting your actions rise up and pass on through you, focusing on the task at hand only. Focusing on the now. Perhaps that is only sensible in his own mind, but it works. It has worked for so very long, and it has gotten him so close to the end.

And yet.

She is slumped in the wavering torchlight, the green and orange of the brazier casting sickly hues across her dirty dress. The ash of the circle is undisturbed. He sees all of this and realises he cannot find that particular place in his mind—the place that has gotten him through so many battles. That place where there is only his task, his service, his goal.

He has been staring at her. He does not know for how long, but he has started to think of all he has done. Of the pact. Of the enemies he has hewn. The scars he bears. The screams and blood and dull horror of his days.

His gaze lingers on that thick hair. The curve of her hips. Her long, white fingers, loose on the dark dirt.

He knows how those hips moved. How those fingers felt, curled in his as they walked.

As they walked, and she smiled, and his son rode high on his shoulders.

The Scythe, surrounded by an army, sits in the flickering torchlight and stares at his wife. He feels his son's small hands tangled in his hair; hears the boy's laugh rain down like music.

As if she knows, she lifts her head. No colour remains in her hair, which used to be as golden as the summer sun. Her face is thinner than it was, too, and pale. Her eyes seem larger, and darker. There is no surprise in them.

"Hello, my love," she says.

He stands over her. He does not remember moving, but he is still outside the ash of the circle.

"Rebecca," he says. It is not a question. He knew her as soon as she came down the path between the trees that morning. They had been far beyond their own lines, deep in enemy territory. She had been alone. Jordan had no idea how the avatar had known where to go, when she would be coming, or that she would not be guarded. She had paused when she saw them, and then raised her hands. Two of his companions had fallen, stiff and silent, and she had been spinning towards a third when the avatar had stepped forward and woven darkness about her. She did something, and the curling blackness started to burn away just as three more men tackled her, held her down and bound her hands in rope woven from the mane of a dead white mare.

He had stood, sword in hand, watching her move, watching her fight. Watching the avatar and the other men take her down. It had not been hesitation or horror or disbelief that had frozen him. It had not been any thought at all. He had simply watched her, drank her in, and then it had been done.

Now, he stands so close, and all that is between them is a thin line of ash and a gulf of years and choices and shame. He wants to ask her so many things, explain so many things, excuse so many things.

But he has his task, his one last day of service, and that means nothing else matters.

Her hands are still bound, but she brings them up together and rubs at her face anyway. He remembers how she used to do that, in the mornings. She would sit up in their bed and yawn, rubbing at her face. Her shoulders would be bare, and he would trace lines on her back. She would squirm when he did.

"Are you the Grey Witch?" he asks. The Grey Witch has been an annoyance for years. Appearing in a battle to turn the ground to a quagmire, or standing on the edge of a camp, dousing fires with a wave of her hand. A year ago she stood on a distant hill and had done something to the dark cloud that hung over the army; it had roiled and shrunk for a day, and late that afternoon, Jordan had heard someone laughing at one of the campfires. But the darkness came back. It always did.

"Would you believe it?" she replies. She almost smiles. It was always a thing with her, that almost-smile.

The Grey Witch is a gnat, a pebble, a thorn. A beautiful thorn, perhaps, not a thorn nonetheless.

He doesn't answer her straight away. It is an old habit, to take his time with one of her questions, to think over what she has said and what she may mean. He remembers all too clearly how quick and bright her mind was—is. Sharper and swifter even than the spear he caught in his hip.

He circles the trap she sits within, circles her words, moves back across the tent. Takes the chair again.

"I think I would," he says finally. "But why? You achieved nothing, and helped no one. You were caught in the end, and easily."

She laughs, just a little, but it's almost too much. It takes him back to sun and warmth and all that is gone. He trembles, on the verge of standing, on the edge of running to her.

Steady, he thinks. *You are almost at the end.*

"People always said you were the best village witch they had ever seen," he goes on. "Even if you weren't powerful enough in the end."

Those words are bitter, and they kill the tremble inside him.

"I don't think anyone could have saved him, Jordan," she murmurs.

"The Dark God can." His voice is steady.

"Oh, my love," she says. "Our boy is gone. He is ash, much like this circle. You know that."

The pyre. The keening. The small body that had not seemed like Christopher at all, not at the end. For a moment her dark eyes reflect those flames, and he sees now that she *is* powerful, and lovely, and fearsome. He sees that she is as clever as always.

But she is also useless.

This whole talk is useless. All that she was to him, all that they were to each other—that is past. Now he has his task, and his bargain. He must stay in the now.

"The Dark God holds agreements with all of his soldiers," Jordan says. "He has never reneged, not once. All know that."

She sits back on her haunches and smooths her hair from her face.

"A boon delivered, after you have served him ten years." Her voice is flat. "And if Christopher is returned, what will you do? Will you hold his hand and tell him of the blood you spilled?"

She shakes her head. "What has been done cannot be undone."

"Are you saying the Dark God won't bring our son back?"

"I'm saying you can't undo the last ten years. Not even a God can turn back time. What will you bring our son back to?" she asks, and now it is her eyes that are wet, her voice that is trembling.

"And what have you done that is any better, with all your skirting around the edges of the muck? You wave your arms at the darkness and then disappear for months, for a year maybe? To what end?"

He snaps his mouth shut before he says more. This is useless. He must stay in the now.

"You are right, " she says, and there is such sorrow, such tiredness in her face. "I have not been powerful enough, not in any of these ten years, no matter what I have tried."

Yes, she tried. Tried for him, he realises. A gnat biting a giant beast, and all for him. That is a shock, but he cannot think on it now.

"We battle on the morrow," he says. "And then the Dark God will grant my boon."

He walks outside and positions himself by the entrance. He stares into the cold and the dark, and does not look back at her. He does not think of her—not her hands, not her hips, not her eyes. Not ten years without her.

Tomorrow, he will bring their son back.

He has miscalculated in battle before. Swearing before the Dark God, promising to serve in his army and to take lives for a decade did not make him immortal or invulnerable or a soldier. He lost the two fingers at the Battle of the Intertwined Springs, and he has a sword-stroke scar across his back that pulls when he runs. There is his aching hip, of course, and a dozen other smaller cuts and mended bones. Over time he became the Scythe, he is the Scythe, and those injuries do not matter.

A blade cares not for the nicks and wear along its edge.

Now he can barely breathe. He has made it back to the camp, back to the tent, but he does not know how. The battle is done, the enemy broken. They had fought with might and courage, but it had not mattered. Here, today and once again, the Dark God will have his way.

He slides from his horse and almost falls. He grasps the reins. His chest feels heavy, and there are bubbles in the blood on his lips. Each breath brings a sucking sound from the edge of his breastplate where the damn pike slipped through. It does not hurt, and in some ways, it is pleasant. A certainty, after so long.

He walks inside, not stumbling, focusing on his shallow breaths. He has not been summoned this time. He wants to see her.

The avatar is in its chair, and his wife, Rebecca, the Grey Witch, sits in her circle. She watches his entrance, unspeaking.

"The Scythe returns," the avatar says, swelling outwards slightly. "Pact fulfilled, and heralding yet another victory."

"You are dying, my love," his wife says. She sounds mildly concerned, as if he had come home from the market with beans that cost too much. The avatar makes no sign of surprise or acknowledgement at her words. So, it had known. Of course it had.

"Yes," he says. "But my task is done. The God will grant my boon."

"She is right, you know," the avatar says. "You are dying. Perhaps you would like to change your request? You could ask to be healed."

"I want my son," Jordan says. Almost a whisper.

"Yes, yes, I know," the avatar says, and the green and orange light flickers a little. It holds up one shadowy tendril-limb, as if forestalling something. "But what is your plan? To die, and leave your child here, with me? Perhaps he could watch the end of your wife? Would a young boy swear to serve, I wonder, for a chance to have one of his parents back? And which of you would he choose?"

The words are worse than his injury. Worse than Rebecca caught, and worse than all he has done and tries not to think of. Of course he should have known. The Dark God never denies a boon, but the Dark God cannot turn back time. Rebecca was right.

Jordan wishes with all of his fading strength to find that place of no-thought. The reaping place, the place of the task and the task only. But that is also the now, and the now has somehow become his past, his wife, his terrible choices again. He breathes, and tries to think of answers to these questions.

"I only ever wanted my son," he whispers, too low to be heard, but the dark creature and the Grey Witch both hear him anyway. He looks at her. "Our son."

"And is that your boon to be granted? Say the words, Jordan the Scythe!" the avatar exclaims, and then laughs, swelling to twice its size in its low chair. The baleful light flickers and dims again. Jordan knows the God, or this thing that is part of the God, will bring his son back, and the boy will be tormented as his father has been. Tormented with blood and with hope, tormented for years if he does not die again, weeping on the battlefield.

His wife regards him steadily with those dark eyes that he loved so much. Those eyes that are so much like Christopher's. He is dying, and his son will come back to serve the Dark God. His wife will watch, and then she will die.

The avatar laughs, and the darkness swells.

"Enough," Rebecca says. She is wearing that almost-smile of hers, although she is crying now, the tears running freely down her cheeks. "Jordan, I have failed, as you have said. But I am here for you now." She holds out her hand.

She has always been the clever one. Wise, always wiser than he. He does not know if she meant to be captured or not, but of course she would somehow be here at the end, when he needed her. When all her other efforts had failed. Her efforts to fight, her efforts for him.

The light flickers again, dims. The avatar waits. Jordan could ask to be healed. He could ask for Rebecca to be free. He falls to his knees, crying, trying to breathe. Their son is gone, and his years of battle, his years of dirtying himself, have done nothing. His wife is here, and he sees the pain in her eyes. He struggles to his feet.

He took himself away for so long. He can give her this.

"I will not," Jordan whispers, Scythe no more. "I will not ask."

He steps across the ash. He pulls his belt dagger and cuts the ropes binding her hands, and then he is in her arms. Light envelopes them, a burning light that is coming from her, from all around, pushing away the darkness in the tent, the darkness in his heart. She has always been powerful, in her own way. It is too much, and it is what he needs. He clings to her as she burns them both.

"Time to go to our son," she whispers in his ear.

Jordan holds his wife, and hopes she is right. He hopes for something after the now.

Farming with Cranky

It's hot. It's always hot. It is cooler up at the other end of the field under the shade of the big trees, but I still prefer it down this end, in the heat. The trees are so big, so dark and mossy and quiet—it's scary. Dad says they grow like that because of the heat. He says that a long time ago it was different.

"You are doing well," he says now, as he wipes sweat from his face and smiles across at me. I sway in my saddle and of course it is right then that I almost fall. I grab at the rough scales, my hands slick with sweat, and I try to sit up straight. I don't need to look back at the house to know Mum will be watching, her hands gripping the yard fence too tightly.

I've been at Dad to let me plough since I saw Mikey next door riding. He went by high on the back of their old Steg, wedged between its back plates and looking all serious, even though I knew he was side-eyeing me the whole time.

"Keep her steady," Dad says. He is on Cranky the Anky, borrowed from Old Johnson for the afternoon. The dopey old thing is almost blind, and happy to just plod along next to the harnessed Trice. I hold on to the reins loosely, like Dad keeps saying, but it's hard. I'm so high up.

"Old man Johnson says they used to use machines to do this," I say.

"Lines are good," Dad says, and that makes me feel pretty good. They are, too. The black earth is turned over in long furrows that fill the air with a rich, dark smell, lines that go all the way up to the huge tangle of forest that marks the end of the reclaimed land. Mikey can side-eye my lines all he wants, he won't do any straighter.

"It's better this way," he says.

"Because the machines made it so hot?"

"We made it hot, honey," Dad replies and wipes his face. "Keep her steady!" he says then, a sudden edge to his voice. I try, but the Trice tosses her head up, snorting, and then gives a little buck. I shriek and scrabble at her knobbly scales with my sweaty hands.

Then Dad is cursing and sliding down from Cranky's back. He is moving so fast he is up the knotted ladder and grabbing me from my saddle before I even really register the roaring.

He slides down, ignoring the ladder, wincing as the Trice's rough hide scrapes his back. For a moment I can feel his heart thudding as he holds me to his side, and then he dumps me on the ground.

"The house! Go!"

There is another roar from the trees, and the Trice snorts and tosses her head. I freeze.

"Go!" Dad shouts again, and I run.

He runs too, but not for the house.

I stumble and then Mum is there, scooping me up like I weigh nothing and ducking back through the narrow yard gate. She puts me down and we both turn, silently frantic, wishing Dad to be safe.

He is rolling right under the fence at the battery when the beast pushes from the dark green world beyond the boundary fence. It looks small because the trees are so huge, but it's really big—big enough to bust through the boundary and charge for Cranky, its horrible mouth gaping, long tail flicking like it has a mind of its own.

"Don't watch," Mum says, and covers my eyes.

There is a humming as Dad reroutes the power to the house fence. Maxing the solar battery only gives enough juice for one big shock, but it is a *really* big one. It would have been better if Dad had gotten the extra charge through the boundary fence in time, but at least we are safe now. Cranky and the Trice are not.

I begin to pull Mum's hand away, but then I think of the Trice, how she stands so patiently when you saddle her, how sometimes she will nuzzle you as you try to harness her. And I think of Cranky, that dopey old thing, plodding along, slow and content under the hot sun. I leave Mum's hand where it is, and my tears are hot against her palm.

Old Johnson looks mad, but then he sighs and rubs his bald head.

"I'll pay the fast track incubation fee," Dad says.

"Ah, don't worry about it." Old Johnson sighs again. "Ain't nobody's fault. And Cranky, he was about done anyways." He rubs his head again. "Your Trice?"

It's Dad's turn to sigh. "We'll manage. We always do."

"Dad," I say. I've been thinking. Thinking about the dark forest that covers most everything. Thinking about what's in there. About why.

"We brought them all back."

He looks down at me, all sweaty and hot and serious, but then he smiles a little bit.

"Yes, honey. A long time ago. They were well suited to how things had gotten. You know that. You've been down to Dobsley's, seen the incubators. Seen the babies."

"I mean we brought them *all* back."

Old Johnson rubs his head again.

"Was hardly anyone left as to object, back then," he says, sounding sour. "Can't say I understand all the decisions that got made. Used to be we were top dogs."

Dad shakes his head and a few drops of sweat fall off his grimy forehead. It's always so hot.

"It's better this way," he says.

Prometheus, Burning

Those damn eagles were made of fire, burning orange and red as they rent and tore. That's not in any of the stories.

I remind myself this you is different. You wearing your white coat and severe expression is not the you that checked me in yesterday, asking all those pointless questions, poking and prodding me. You are not the you that brought my food, or the you that mopped my floor last night. It is hard, because you are all so fleeting, lovely sparks that spin and flash and go before you flash again.

"Mr..." you begin, and then inspect your clipboard like you are unsure. I know you are not.

"Mr P," you finish. "Don't have a name?"

"I do," I say. "Lots of them."

Your smile is professionally plastic, your pale eyes sharp, your hair grey and short. You are very different, yes, your own tiny spark. This room is different, this time is different. This space is very white and smells of ammonia, and it is such a strange thing to associate that acrid smell with cleanliness. Once, when I was treated in an asylum for a malady of the mind that burned in its own special way, when you applied treatments of dunking and shock and hard cane floggings that did not work but were called advancements, that smell was mixed with dirt and sweat and brokenness. Now, it is the crisp scent of efficiency and sterility.

"Do you know what we do here?" you ask.

"You play with fire," I answer. I don't mean to, but sometimes I grow tired of the smiles and the handwaving and the lies. You have so little time to share the truth, and you do not recognise it. It is charming and frustrating and a thing I have always struggled with, because I love you so. All of you.

You look shocked, your lined skin wrinkling more on your forehead, your gaze narrowing.

"I don't know where you heard that," you say. "Here we do cutting-edge therapy and research."

You are angry with me, as you so often are.

"Yes," I say, and it is the wrong thing.

I love you in your white coat and anger. I love you as you pass by outside in your blue janitor overalls, whistling. I loved you yesterday, the dark haired nurse with cold hands. I loved you when you walked the streets of Genoa amongst the corpses, wearing your long doctor-beaked mask and coming to bleed me every day, trying to let the fire out.

But love has never given me the right words.

"You are very lucky to be here," you say, curtly.

"Lucky," I repeat.

Perhaps your face softens. "We take on only the most interesting, most rare cases. We will do tests. We may be able to treat you."

I say nothing. I burn so within.

I dream of the eagles. They come out of the east and they are screaming in the agony of their own burning, which becomes my burning as they rend and tear and gorge themselves on me in a frenzy. I scream, because I know this is only the start of my punishment. My crime of love, my gift of fire, will be met in kind. Love and fire will be my curse.

"You need to tell us where you are from," you say. You are angry again, and I cannot help my smile. You were like this after Nagasaki, when my body decayed, hot with radiation, but would not succumb. After Strasbourg and all the dancing, when so many collapsed and I had danced on for so long, my feet raw and bleeding, my face red and sweating, my blood boiling and roaring in my ears.

Always the anger. Always the puzzlement, the frustration. You would not believe, the times I succumbed and told you. Any of you.

You tap your clipboard with your pen, hard. There are many notes there now, thick pages of results and summaries and your wonderings, no doubt.

"You have antibodies to things that have not existed for ages. You have markers of diseases we have never encountered, evidence of other things. Pock marks, faded but there. Radiation lesions. Small but extremely deep burn scars around your midriff. Have you ever been burned, Mr P?"

"Oh yes," I say. "Lots."

It is not like the stories. There is no strong mortal to save me, no hero who brings the eagles low and breaks my chains. My torture will never end, and it will change and change again.

One day the eagles do not come in their screaming forms. Despite everything, I feel a moment of hope as the chariot of the sun rises in the east, only to have it die as small arrows of orange flame wing their way towards me. They alight, and they burrow, my pain still the size of the world but turned small, eating down and down into me. I feel it anew—my gift of fire, turned to my curse. I will carry it with me, as to what purpose I am unsure. I am afraid.

My chains break. There is no need of them now.

I am a puzzle and you were ever curious, every one of you.

"Your immune system is a mess," you tell me. "We've tested you again and again. If you had even one of the diseases or conditions indicated, you should be dead. In some cases, years ago. Centuries even."

You don't expect an answer, because you cannot imagine one. That is good, because I say the wrong thing so often, and the truth is one of these.

"But you do have the markers for Syca-15," you say, naming the new fire within, the one that drew your attention. You enjoy your names so. "Which is why we took you. We have several new treatments we can try, if you are willing."

This is how it goes. Sometimes the fire within is triggered from without—radiation, plague, air-borne viruses. Then my body burns and writhes. Sometimes those burrowing, buried flickers of eagle ignite on their own, twisting, chewing, changing me from within. Either way, you eventually come, to soothe, to calm. Or at least to try.

I gave you fire, which you have moulded and shaped, and now you use it to quell the flames within me. Sometimes you get it wrong. Leeching blood, beating with sticks. More poison rather than antidote. But I endure, and eventually you get it right.

"You can try," I say.

I wander far from my cliff, flinching with every sunrise, hiding from every bird. There are not many of you, and when I see you, you are huddled around my gift in small groups, searing meat, baking coarse loaves, warming yourselves. I feel the flame eagles within, and I want to flee far from you, but I cannot. I love you so, so I linger, and linger overlong, hanging on the edges of you, wanting to see you progress. I try to ignore the stirrings of the eagles.

The first time I grow sick I know immediately it is the first of many burnings. I writhe on the forest floor, delirious and babbling with fever until you find me. You take me to your small hut and give me some sort of broth, dark and thick. It cools me, calms me.

"My mother taught me this," you say. "Boiling the leaves over a flame brings out the goodness."

I am cured, but not. I can feel the flames within, deep, small, waiting.

Yes. There is no need of my chains now.

The white walls are unchanging, the smell of sterility as harsh as ever. The only track of the days is your tiredness, which creeps and creeps with every vial of blood drawn, every pin prick or reaction charted. Your anger too, grows, your words shorter, your gaze sharper. You stop carrying your clipboard. You spend long moments glaring at me as if I insult you with who I am, the answers I withhold. I can feel the eagles stirring, the Syca-15—which is just another name for burning—rising.

Until one day you are different. Your brow is clear, your clipboard back in hand. And I know your fire has met mine and matched it, at least for now.

"You have a treatment," I say. This is how it goes, more often now than in years past when you sometimes fumbled and missed the mark. When you had to try again and again for understanding, for something new, to cast your fire into a shape that would serve. Now you have turned it into a million tools. You advance so much, so quickly, as I wished for you in the beginning.

"Perhaps," you say, and then bite your lip.

"Truth is, I think I've had a treatment for your Syca-15 for maybe a week. I've held off on it though."

This is new, but I do not speak, for fear of what I would say.

"I don't know who you are," you say. "But... you are like a tapestry of ills. So many things inside of you. There has to be a root cause."

You pause, as if to judge my shock or response. Still I say nothing. Anything would be a wrong thing.

"It took a lot of doing," you say. "But I think I found something. You..." you sigh. Shake your head. "You have some sort of heat signature, something in your liver. It's very hard to detect. It is very small, and it... flickers."

This is indeed new. I could tell you of the rending, the biting and clawing. I could tell you how, in my dreams, I am back on the cliff, watching the eagles turn to fire, burrow inside.

"It's fire," I say.

"I could treat it, I think," you say, as if you have not really heard me. "I might be able to develop a therapy."

Perhaps you can save me. Perhaps you are my strong mortal, come finally to slay the eagles with syringe and solutions rather than bow and arrows. Perhaps this is what I have been waiting for for so long. For you to best my fire with your own, completely.

You smile. It is a smile of relief and of triumph, a smile I have seen before. A smile I saw when that first broth eased my fever. When you treated my swollen and bleeding feet with herbs and honey wraps after I finally collapsed from the dancing plague. When you shrunk my tumours with harsh chemicals, when you injected me with those first clumsy antibiotics.

Every time you fought the fire within me with the fire I gave you. When you applied a salve that would help so many afterwards.

I am still giving. You use me, treat me, cure me, and still I burn for you. I burn for all of you. It is a gift.

Finally, I find the right words.

"No," I say. "I'd rather you didn't."

Diamonds are Forever

They are coming in pretty close to the event horizon. Fast, too.

"I still say it's a stupid name," Theo says. That is usually good for either a laugh or an argument, but this time Yanic just nods without looking up from his console.

"You know, because it's not a horizon, not really. I like *transition zone*, because it implies a gradation. What we're doing wouldn't work if it wasn't a gradation," Theo tries.

Nothing.

"Come on, man, lighten up. Everything is going like it should."

That is maybe unfair. Theo is nominally the Captain of their two-person crew, but really he is just the pilot. Yanic is the payload specialist with his weird combination of astrophysics and geology and long list of other things—an off-the-chart genius. He has to be, to be saving everyone. Or expanding the world. Or advancing human-kind to the stars. Or all of the above.

He is also usually good company. He waxes a bit philosophical about everything, but Theo likes that. Otherwise Yanic is laidback. Practical. Easy to spend time with in their cramped quarters. But sending a string of giant nano-fibre sheaths skimming through the upper reaches of a singularity's transition zone to crush coal into diamond lattices is stressful.

Especially since they only have one shot.

Theo should be just as stressed. They need to whip the trailing sheaths of coal into the right trajectory, and doing so without getting spaghettified is no mean feat. Particularly since next they have to swing their little ship around the edge of the danger zone to catch the new lattices as they come out of the deflection arc. But Theo is good at plotting trajectories and flight paths and it's all been programmed.

"Sorry, Theo," Yanic says, and forces a smile. "Pointy end of things, you know? I wanted to recheck the Osmium layering and the probabilities of photon cage production as the coal bundles are crushed."

"Yanic, you've done nothing but fuss over the console for hours," Theo replies. "Why don't you leave off?"

Yanic bites his lip.

"Do you ever wonder how different it would have been? If we had worked out the quantum reverberations of Osmium-diamond lattices earlier? Before we had mined out the few natural reserves of high quality diamonds and cut them all up for jewellery, made them unusable because we wanted something that looked pretty?"

This again. Theo has no idea why Yanic keeps coming back to this, when they both agree. It's hard not to, when Earth is limping along and the few people that are left are all no doubt staring upwards, wondering how the two of them are faring. Hoping for deliverance from above.

"We didn't cut them all up," Theo says, because they do have one decent diamond lattice. It is embedded in their ship's quantum drive, and it's the only reason they could reach this black hole. It's also given them their last chance—flying out here to skim the last of Earth's anthracitic coal across the transition zone to crush it into new lattices for more quantum drives.

"And the rest of the coal," Yanic continues, as if he hasn't heard Theo. "We chewed through it centuries ago. Just like we've used everything else."

Sure. They've talked about it enough. If they hadn't screwed around so much back at home they wouldn't be so desperate. But now is not the time.

"Deployment in three minutes," Theo says. Yanic is not going to cheer up until it is done. "Do you want to check your calculations again?"

The sheaths are whipping their way through the upper transition zone and the ship is well on course to intercept the new diamond lattices, but Yanic is still worried. He keeps checking the console, the deflection arc, the timing.

"Come on," Theo says. "Drink your coffee. It's reconstituted warm muck, but it's also the best brew for fifteen hundred light years."

"Do you really think we are doing the right thing?" Yanic asks, without sucking on his straw. "We've used the only diamond lattice left on Earth to get out here so we can crush coal into more lattices, and for what? So we can go mining for more lattices, more coal, more everything, on some other world? Worlds?"

“What do you propose?” Theo asks, for the hundredth time since they launched. “There’s nothing much left on Earth. It’s not exactly pleasant back there.”

“But that’s just it!” Yanic says. “Look at all this!” He waves around at their little ship, which is mostly just the quantum drive under their feet, some cramped bunks behind a bulkhead, and at the end of a short, sealable corridor, enough of a cargo bay to hold the new lattices. “We built this when we have so little, when there are so few of us. We can do so much when we really need to, and we’re just going to bug out? Leave Earth?”

“Hardly,” Theo says, although he knows his words are hollow even as he speaks. “We will bring resources back to Earth after the new ships go out. You know we will.”

“Yeah,” Yanic says, his mouth twisting. “And if we do, that will fix everything.”

Theo doesn’t know what to say to that, but he doesn’t have to because something starts beeping.

“What’s that?” Yanic asks.

“I decided to run a forecast of the arc against the actual trajectory of the sheaths,” Theo says, turning to his console. He may not be a polymath, but he is good at checking flight patterns. “The angle is off. The lattices are slowing too much. They won’t escape the pull of the singularity.”

There is a second of silence.

“We will have to leave them,” Yanic says.

Theo can’t tell if Yanic sounds happy or not, but it doesn’t matter. Theo is already moving the ship.

The whole ship is shuddering as the quantum drive fights the draw of the singularity.

"You can't take us in there, we'll die!" Yanic shouts. It's been almost five minutes since Theo altered course, and Yanic has been shouting for most of that time.

"This is our only chance!" Theo tells him this time, instead of just yelling at him to shut up again. There is no more coal back on Earth. No diamonds. Not enough Osmium. Not enough of anything.

"It's not!" Yanic screams from his seat an arm's length away. "Earth is our chance!"

"Shut up!" Theo shouts back. "We're here now, and I'm a bit busy!"

They are almost in position. Theo can deploy the lines, and if the sheaths are still intact, they can still be caught. He just needs to compensate for the drag of the singularity and the ship shudder and the decaying trajectory of the sheaths while aligning the ship's velocity appropriately and God knows what else.

And he could really do without the shouting.

It's done. There were a few moments where Theo thought the lines would not catch, and then would not hold, but while they were strained they had not broken. The sheaths are now in, they are out of the transition zone, and all Theo needs to do is confirm the homeward course from their new position. Yanic has gone to the cargo bay to do a check on the new lattices and Theo is drinking a double bagful of faux-espresso. It will leave him short on the home run but what the hell—he's earned it.

He brings up the course subroutines on his console and pauses with his mouth full of warm, bitter liquid. He is looking at the master trajectory file. It has been modified recently. Far too recently. The wrong angle, the angle that dropped the sheaths too close to the singularity, is right there in the equations.

Yanic.

Theo unclips and pushes himself backwards. Towards the cargo bay, towards the corridor control panel.

Yanic is coming out of the cargo bay as Theo reaches the near end of the corridor. Yanic looks at Theo, and that is enough. They both know what the other knows.

Yanic gives Theo a pained little smile. He closes the cargo bay door behind him and comes down the corridor.

"I'm going to jettison the whole bay," he says. "It would've been easier if the trajectory failed, but this way we can say it was a ship integrity issue."

Theo closes and seals the corridor door between them and punches in the Captain's emergency override. There will be no jettisoning of anything for Yanic.

Yanic comes close to the little porthole style window in the door. He shakes his head and presses the comms button on his side of the door.

"Theo," he says, his voice coming down from above, from all around. "We can't keep on like this. If we spread out, move out from Earth, we will do what we have already done. Take and take. You know we will. And we will do it over and over."

Theo punches his own comms button.

"You don't think people have learned?" he asks. "No one on Earth is living in luxury right now. Everyone knows the folly of the past."

"Do they?" Yanic asks. He shakes his head roughly. "Then what are we doing here?"

Theo has no answer for that. Nothing that doesn't feel weak, that doesn't feel like an empty justification. At best, a reaching hope.

But there are so many people waiting for them.

"We can't make that decision," Theo says instead. "It's too final."

"What we are doing on Earth is final!" Yanic says, and he has tears in his eyes now. Theo can feel the same threatening him.

"We need to take the lattices back," Theo tries. "We can talk then. Make our case to everyone."

Again—weak. "It's not our decision to make," Theo says again, but this time he doesn't know who he is saying it to.

"It has to be our decision!" Yanic cries, and wipes his face. "Your decision. This is it, Theo. We can go home and look to ourselves because we finally, finally have no choice. God, we are flying around a black hole compressing coal into diamond lattices for quantum drives! Do you really think we would have no hope of changing things on Earth if we really tried, if we had no other options? Or we can go home and turn our eyes upwards. Turn our grasping hands to the stars. How long will it take before we are back in this position again? Before we have sucked up every damn resource we can reach?"

"Not for millennia," Theo says. But Yanic is right. Eventually they will be just as desperate again. After many more worlds. After many more Earths.

Yanic says nothing else, just stares through the glass, tears on his cheeks.

Theo could open the door. They could jettison the cargo. Go back to Earth as a failed mission and see what they can do when there truly were no other options.

Or Theo can leave Yanic in the corridor. Keep the override on, and take the lattices home. Give them over to so many people who are waiting. Who want them. Who need them. Who are desperate.

His hand hovers over the control panel, and Theo realises Yanic is right about one thing, at least.

It's his decision to make.

Goldbergian Physics

There was junk all over the lab bench.

"Clarence? Clarence!"

But the janitor was right there, next to the fridge the students kept their lunches in. Professor Stanislov stared at the man's long, oddly thin grey head and watched him blink with several eyelids. There was something odd about Clarence, but the Professor just couldn't think of what it was.

"There you are. What is all this?"

"I'll clean it up right away, Professor."

Stanislov almost told Clarence to forget it. He didn't need the bench space, so it shouldn't really matter if the new janitor used it. He frowned, trying to think of when the janitor had started work. But then his gaze drifted to the whiteboard, his computations and equations, and he sighed.

"Problems, Professor?"

He turned back to Clarence. The blue overalls made sense, but the man was very tall, and grey, and really, how many eyelids did one person need? He was also not cleaning the bench. He seemed to be talking to the fridge instead.

"I know this way is more difficult, but the personality scan was clear—if we just tell him the answer it may trigger—what do they call it? Performance issues. And besides, we decided no more, ah, borrowing of individuals from their locations."

"Just stuck a bit, is all," the Professor said. Clarence's fridge conversation somehow didn't seem that important. Instead, he found himself staring at the mess on the bench. There was a long piece of plastic tubing propped up across several tissue boxes. There was also something like a small windmill made out of bent paperclips and tape, and a set of new pencil erasers standing tall, like dominoes. After that, an assortment of other things—a tub of water balanced on a raised wooden ruler, a string attached to a spoon, other office flotsam—all of it interconnected in some way. Sticking off the side of the bench next to it all were a series of rectangular frames made from ballpoint pens, one above the other, each with a canopy of tissue paper taped to it.

"Stuck on what, Professor?"

Stanislov glanced at the fridge. Idly, he wondered what would be inside if he opened it. For some reason he really didn't want to do that.

"What do you like about being a janitor, Clarence?"

The grey-skinned Clarence smiled slightly.

"Well, I am kind of new to it. But I guess you could say I like things to be neat and tidy. It's actually something everyone likes to do, where I am from. Help get things squared away."

Stanislov nodded. "That is what I like about physics. The neatness of it. A place for everything. Except..." He fell silent, and then sighed. Again.

"I've been working on this muon-based adaptation of the standard model for what seems forever. I feel like the answer is right there, but I can't see it."

Clarence nodded. "Sounds frustrating. And I bet"—and here he glanced at the fridge—"that you would hate it if someone just told you the answer."

Stanislov actually shuddered. "Oh, that would be horrible."

"See?" the janitor said. He appeared to be addressing the fridge again, which made an odd sound. Maybe it needed re-gassing or something, Stanislov thought.

"Haven't muons been in the news lately?" Clarence asked.

"Oh, yes indeed," Stanislov nodded. "Quite exciting stuff—the work out of Fermilab and other places suggesting the magnetism of muons is much more than expected. Funny you should mention it—it is what has been causing me so much grief." He waved at the whiteboard. "I started with the recent work on charge-conjugation and parity-reversal violation. Those findings come close to explaining why there is more matter than antimatter in the universe."

"If you say so," Clarence said. The fridge made another odd noise. Clarence shushed it.

"At first I thought the magnetism results for muons was exactly what I needed. But it actually makes the calculations impossible." Stanislov shook his head. "I was so close."

Clarence held up a small marble between his long, grey fingers. "Sometimes when I build my little contraptions, I like to think of this as my problem, moving towards a solution. Maybe for you it can be matter, or the universe or something." He placed the marble in the plastic tube and gave it a little flick.

Stanislov watched the marble roll to the end of the tube. There it got caught in the paperclips of the windmill, which spun around to deposit it against the first eraser. This fell, knocking the others, the last of which landed on the balanced ruler. The tub of water tipped. Stanislov almost smiled as office equipment and tape and pencils and other things moved and bumped and shifted, until, eventually, the original marble was knocked once more, rolling off the bench onto the first thin canopy of tissue paper. It sat for a moment before there was a soft tearing sound, and then it fell through to the next tissue paper just below. The process repeated several more times, until finally, the marble hit the floor. Stanislov stared, his mouth hanging open.

"The marble is not the universe," he said slowly. "The tissue paper is." He looked at the strange janitor, his eyes wide. "Stacked Universes with uneven cycling of matter and anti-matter, driven by muon magnetism. That would explain why I haven't been able to solve my equations. Oh my God."

Clarence smiled just a little. "If you say so, Professor. You're the expert, after all. I just like things to be neat and tidy."

The Plumber

"You may as well be a plumber," the woman said, as if he had said he was a sex offender. The others at the table looked similarly unimpressed. One humanoid, his skin mottled green, sniffed delicately and turned away.

Jax said nothing. The group looked like the typical mix, the same as the previous testing levels. Scientists and social scientists, anthropologists and extra-terrestrial theorists. Probably at least one political scientist. Some had biomods, extra limbs, or plug-ports. One had what looked like an overly large pulsing golden eye on top of its bald head. The only trait they had in common was arrogance—it oozed out of them. You said "technician", and they thought you had said "servant". *Screw them all,* Jax thought. He had made it through the previous tests, just like them. The lights dimmed slightly and the holoview started up, turning them all a little green in the soft glow.

"Simulation: training and testing module six point nine five. Attend." The voice was clipped and neutral, almost nasal. The group settled and grew silent. This was the final test. Not all of them would get through, but some might.

"Simulation: biohazard. Type, humanoid with reptilian and arachnid DNA. Intelligence: low. Resilience: extreme."

There was a pause, followed by an audible click. "Threat level: real."

There was a moment of silence, and then chaos erupted in the room. The woman who had spoken before leapt up, shaking her head. "No, no, I did not agree to this!"

Others were making similar protests. The man with the pulsing golden eye was banging on the locked door. Jax sat quietly. They all had, in point of fact, agreed, but he doubted many of them had read the fine print. It had been the same at the lower testing levels. They thought the expedition would be an adventure, something for their resumes. None of them had questioned why there were no applicants with previous experience—they had all opted out of this one. He had known better. The mission was deemed critical, and applicants would be expendable.

The voice came again. "Simulation started. Attend."

A hush fell over the room as they all strained to hear. At first there was nothing, and then, faintly, a scraping sound, followed by a chittering. There was a scrabbling, like something trying to gain purchase, and then silence again. The green humanoid turned to say something to the woman, and there was a loud banging sound, followed by a screech. A serrated claw burst through the titanium lined door, rending downwards, tearing it like it was paper. It withdrew and smashed through again, widening the hole. A cluster of small red eyes peered through, and Jax got a glimpse of greenish black scales and thick muscles lining a long neck. He saw its mouth open and close, saw the bulging sacks within.

"Get back!" he yelled, but it was too late. The creature smashed its head through the narrow opening, pushing this way and that to widen the gap. It opened its mouth and sprayed acrid liquid. The green humanoid went down, writhing. The man with the golden eye shrank back, trying to hide under the table. Two others were screaming at the holoview, their voices overlapping, nothing but noise.

Jax squinted. Arachnid, reptilian, humanoid. He could see the bulging vessels running just under the scales, feeding the venom sacks. He wracked his brain. Humanoid, but extremely resilient. Still, *humanoid*. He looked at the bulging vessels again, running down the neck. They were in roughly the right spot, and near the surface.

He stepped forward and snatched up a piece of titanium. The creature screamed and pushed its head further into the room and Jax slipped to one side, waiting. It withdrew its head and worked on the door more with its serrated claws. It began chittering again.

"What are you doing?" the woman screamed at him. He gestured for her to shut up.

The creature pushed its head through again. This time it was far enough in, but the angle was wrong. Jax looked at the woman, waved at her again. "I need you to move. Get its attention," he whispered.

She shook her head and shrank down behind the desk, crowding in near the others who had huddled there. The creature spotted the movement and thrust forward, twisting its head. The sacks bulged once more. It was now or never.

Jax stuck the shard of titanium into its neck, thrusting as hard as he could. The scales were hard, and he felt like he had hit a ceramic tiled wall. The titanium skittered along the surface, leaving a white scratch mark, and then dug in slightly.

Slightly was enough. Blood spewed out, mixed with the vile liquid the thing had been pumping into its sacks. Jax jerked his hand back quickly, avoiding the gush of blood and acid. The creature screamed and withdrew from the mangled door. There was the sound of violent thrashing in the hallway, and then all was still. Silence filled the room.

"Simulation complete," the clipped voice spoke into the silence.

The woman stepped forward. "How did you know to do that?" she asked, her eyes wide.

Jax smiled. "Like I said, I'm a technician. A bio-engineering technician," he shrugged. "It's all just plumbing, really."

Love and Thorns

The room is as bland and beige as any hospital room, the air full of disinfectant and the clinging scent of endings. Bobby brushes at a blue butterfly that hovers near his face as a large orange and black one lands near the door. Green vines come to life, sprouting from the flat frame near the creature's delicate feet. They curl towards him, thorns budding and bristling along their lengths before it all fades away.

His eyes widen. His father never used to make thorns.

They sit at the kitchen table, where the two of them take their meals. They have sat here night after night for years, sometimes talking, sometimes silent as Bobby's father works. It has always been Bobby's favourite room, and his favourite time.

His father likes gardens and trees and earth. Butterflies and flowers and the smell of green life. For years, Bobby has watched his father practice, making small, reaching plants that spread across the side bench, heavier ferns curling from the cupboard edges, and tiny lizards darting around the sugar bowl. He has spent so much time watching the space bloom and grow and change. First, he watched it all with wonder. Later, with anticipation.

Now, with neither.

"You don't have to do this," his father says, not for the first time. "Not for me."

Some people call Bobby's father The Life Maker. Some call him The Master of Beauty, although he is not handsome. His dark hair is coarse. His lips are wide, his eyes small, his eyebrows so twisted and bushy they should be ridiculous, and yet they are not. He is a man who makes wonders with a wave of his hand and always speaks softly. With Bobby, especially.

"It's what I want," Bobby says, because he can't speak the truth. He can't say that everything he does, everything he tries, *is* for this man. He can't say that all he wants is not to fail.

"Try again, then," his father says quietly.

Bobby closes his eyes. His task is simple enough: make a patch of sunlight fall across the table, even though the curtains are drawn and the afternoon is dull. It should be the easiest thing—just light, not matter, not movement. A simple trick, a passing illusion with no substance.

Bobby wants it badly, wants to feel what it's like to make something—yes, he wants that. But mostly he wants to see his own light shine across his father's face. He wants to illuminate his father's smile with his own creation. His father is watching patiently, but with a rare, slight frown.

Bobby tries. He delves deep. He wants nothing else in that moment.

Nothing happens.

"It's okay," his father says, as that soft smile of his smooths the frown away. "It's really okay."

"You can't be in here."

Bobby starts. A nurse sits on the far side of the bed, beyond the figure he has been trying not to look at.

"I'm his...ah, my name is Bobby. Robert, I mean. He's my father."

The words are hard to say. The nurse stares, her features drawing downwards slowly, as if Bobby is a weight pulling her towards the ground.

His father stirs, but Bobby doesn't turn to him. Not yet.

"I'll be back soon," the nurse says as she moves from the bedside. Her words are full of her judgement. He has been absent, and now he is here, so very late. Too late, really.

He holds the door open for her.

His wrist aches.

Bobby sits at his desk. Today's tears are drying on his face. He still can't make sunlight. He has tried and tried, and it's supposed to be easy. His fists are clenched, and his stomach aches like it's full of hot stones. He is a failure. His father says it is okay, that it doesn't matter, but it does. To Bobby it matters more than anything to give this to his father, the man who has given him so much.

But...his father does not often do sunlight. He makes living things. Soft and growing things, budding and new. Flowers and jewelled dragonflies and the passing feel of misty rain on the skin, these are the things his father loves.

So...a flower, perhaps. A red rose, heavy with dew and that scent that is so like Bobby's faded memory of his mother's skin. Bobby stares at his desk, and thinks of the red petals. Of the smooth feel of them between his fingers. Of how his father will smile when he sees the red certainty of the bloom. He thinks of how he will succeed, and how he will be like his father after all.

Nothing happens.

"Useless!" he spits, and his clenched fists tighten until his fingernails cut into his palms.

He can't do anything. He stares down at his whitened, trembling fists as hot tears rise. Pointless tears, as pointless as the rest of him. And suddenly the ache that has been growing inside him, those hot stones in his stomach, are so burning and sour and heavy he cannot hold it all in.

A tendril bursts from the desktop. Not a rose. Not a flower, but a twisting thing, thickening quickly and moving towards him. It is not the fresh green of a growing plant. It is a sickly, brownish-yellow, gnarled and crooked and hard even as it moves. It wraps around his hand and then his wrist, tightening. It squeezes, and then the thorns come, long and curved and piercing his skin hungrily.

He screams.

Bobby's father struggles to prop himself up on his pillow. His hair is not dark and coarse now, but thin and grey and stuck in strands to his pale scalp. He smiles, and it is full of love and horrible to see after so long.

"You've come," his father rasps.

A paper cup of water with a plastic straw sits on the dresser, and Bobby brings it to him. He sips greedily, almost frantically for a moment, his dark eyes bright.

"That's better," he says. He lays back, tired from the small effort, and Bobby's eyes sting.

"They called me," Bobby says. He doesn't say he had been planning on contacting his father. It would sound fake, like a nothing thing to push away the awkwardness, even though it is true.

"I'm so sorry," his father says.

"I'm so sorry," Bobby's father says from his seat at the kitchen table. He has finished bandaging Bobby's wrist. Tears rim his eyes, and none of his creations enliven the room. The kitchen is just a kitchen, for the first time in a long time.

Except for the thick tendril of vine that lies between them on the table. The thorns are long and wicked, each still red with Bobby's blood.

His father's gaze drops to the tendril. "This...this is my fault." His voice breaks on the last word, and he draws in a shuddering breath.

Bobby's wrist aches. He doesn't want to look at the thorns. Each is so long and sharp they must have scraped his bone.

But still...

"What do you mean?" he asks. "I made that. I did it, and it is more than just light. It is real."

"I know," his father says, and there is a pain in his words that mirrors the feeling in Bobby's wrist. He looks at his son, and his tears spill down his cheeks.

"What we do..." He hesitates, touches his chest with one shaking hand, and then touches the same hand to Bobby's cheek. "It...it comes from inside."

Bobby doesn't understand. He stares at his father. The soft smile, so often on his face, is gone. Bobby looks down at the vine. The yellow-brown thickness of it. The bloodied thorns, long and solid and razor sharp. His wrist throbs, dull and hot.

He could not do what his father wanted, but he could do...this. He made something, even though he was sure he was useless. Even though it hurt.

"I just need practice," he says. That yellow, woody tendril, it could be more. It could be better.

He could be better.

But his father is shaking his head. "No," he says. "Nothing good will come from that. I don't think this is what you want. Not truly."

He looks more than sorry. He looks bereft. "Let's both take some time away from this. No more practice for now. I want you to promise me."

Bobby clutches his aching wrist with his free hand. He made the vine. It hurt him, but he did it.

And he does want this. He wants it for his father. He wants to make all the things his father loves so. But he can't say that. He just can't.

Bobby nods.

"You came back," his father says, gaze feverish as he sits propped against his pillows. "You came so I could make things right."

The words are sharper than any thorns could be. Bobby almost recoils, and he clutches his wrist. The scars are old now, but are thicker than they were, overlapping, tight and shining.

It took him a long time to stop completely.

"You have nothing to apologise for," Bobby says.

His father smiles, and it is not soft. It is sharp and curved and not for Bobby at all. It is turned inwards. Bobby knows all about that.

His father stands in the doorway to Bobby's room, his face pale and pained.

Bobby pulls his sleeve down, but it is pointless. There is too much blood. There is always too much blood when he practices.

"How long have you been doing this?" his father asks. His eyes shift from Bobby's arm to the thick coil of sickly vines on the desk. The thorns are long and dark and have done their work, like they always do.

Bobby is sick with the pain. He's sure he can turn things around. He can move away from these painful things he makes, but he needs more practice. He can be what his father always wanted him to be, even if it hurts to learn. It will be worth it. Worth the ache in his wrist. Worth his flesh pierced over and over, his blood on the desk and on the floor.

"I'll keep trying," he says instead of answering. "I can do it."

"Son, you can't," his father says, and the words cut through Bobby, sharper and more painful than anything else.

"I'm not useless!" he shouts, because that is what it feels like when the thorns cut—*useless*, the word inside the throbbing heat, inside the ache, repeating over and over.

It is too much. He can't be here. He can't turn these sickly vines into something beautiful with his father looking at him like that.

He has to get out.

"Why didn't you tell me you were sick?" Bobby asks. It comes out sounding like an accusation, but Bobby doesn't know which of them it is really aimed at.

His father's smile turns from that horrid, sharp thing to something like the old, soft expression. A rose rather than a thorn, but different than it used to be. A flower that hides the sharpness just below, perhaps.

I did that, Bobby thinks.

"You grew thorns because of me, you know," his father says in that raspy, dry voice. He lifts one hand and gestures at Bobby's wrist. The scars there are like a silver bracelet of harm, of bitterness and effort. But they are also old now.

"No," Bobby says, his own voice dry.

"Yes, son," his father says, and his hand rises just a little more. A thick and twisted tendril blooms on the IV stand and races down to his father's arm. It twists around his withered wrist, sudden short thorns biting, beads of bright red rising there among older scars. Then the vine and thorns fade, leaving nothing but fresh wounds behind.

"They have been part of everything since you left," his father says.

"Please don't leave," his father says. They are in the kitchen, of course, but neither of them is sitting. Bobby stands in the doorway with his suitcase. Just the bare essentials, really, but the thing is still heavy enough to make his wrist hurt.

The cuts are deep, and he hasn't learned how to make fewer thorns; sometimes he thinks there are more every time he tries. But it will be different when he leaves. When he stops thinking of his father's soft smile, of how he is failing his father over and over.

"I'll do it, you know," Bobby says. "I'll learn how to do more."

"Is that what you really want?" his father asks, and the question twists itself into Bobby and wraps itself around his heart. The feeling is tight, and sharp, and not something he wants to think about.

"Of course it is," he says, and snatches up his suitcase. He turns and leaves without looking back, without seeing the pain in his father's face.

Bobby came with things to say, but as he stares at his father's thorns, he says something else.

"I did this to you," he says.

He doesn't mean this room, or his father's thinning hair and rasping voice, but the silvery scars on his wrist—yes, those.

"No," his father says in that way of old. The patient way. The soft way. "I did this to myself, I think."

That hurts to hear, because that is what Bobby had realised he needed to say as well. What he had been planning on saying when he reached out. Before the hospital called. He stares at his father's wrist, and then at his own. That thick ring of scars, the shining, twisting remnants of what he thought he needed. What he thought he wanted. He holds it up to his father.

"I did this to myself, too," he says. He doesn't know if it is true or not. It is all mixed up, what they did to themselves, what they did to each other. But suddenly he is crying, and his father is smiling his old smile through his own tears.

They reach for each other, clasping hand to wrist, scars to fingertips. Red roses bloom, heavy with scent and dew-laden, spreading across the bed, the blankets, the walls.

There are no thorns.

Better World

Marty is maybe twenty people from the teal void that fills the humming doorframe when he waves to the woman with the clipboard. She is wearing a grey suit and her hair is cut short. She smiles as she comes over.

"I don't think I can do this," he says. He keeps his voice low, but the twenty-something girl in front of him turns and raises one eyebrow. She's kind of cute with her spiky hair, and that makes him feel like an idiot.

"Of course," the woman says. She scans her clipboard, and then gestures to a small, much more regular door in the side wall. "Follow me please, Mr Tims."

She walks fast enough that he has to hurry after. Most people ignore him, because their heads are full of what is in front of them. There is a man a few people ahead with a little girl in his arms. His face is creased with old worry. He stares at the front of the line while his daughter watches Marty with too-wide eyes.

The woman is right to hurry. His lack of conviction is best not displayed to the others being processed here at Better World.

There are a couple of comfy chairs placed close together, and there is a generic print of a waterfall on the wall. Marty wonders if it's an image from the other side. It could be.

There is a door in the far wall with an exit sign above it, which makes sense. It would not be great to have to go back past the others to leave.

As Marty sits there is a thin cheer from the main room.

"Sometimes that happens," the woman says as she sits in the other chair. "When the first one or two from a larger group go through."

Marty doesn't reply. He should be out there cheering. People who put their name in, they want this. Most are desperate for it, in one way or another. He thought he had been as well.

"Don't worry, Mr Tims," the woman says, and smiles a clipboard holder's smile. "This happens as well. It's a big thing to process, being one of the lucky ones."

Now there is a small wail from behind them—the little girl, no doubt. It stops abruptly, likely cut off by the colour teal.

"What's your main concern?" she asks, still with the smile.

"Have you been through?" he asks, which is stupid.

"You know I haven't. No one can go through and come back."

"I still don't understand that," Marty says.

"See ya soon!" Someone calls from the next room. It sounds a lot like a twenty-something girl, upbeat and confident. There is some muted laughter. He would be going through next, if he were out there. The line is moving fast.

Clipboard lady spreads her hands. "I don't either. I'm not a physicist. Quantum transfer of consciousness means people can't come back, whatever that means. And we still have trouble with live feeds and most forms of communication. But you've seen the stills, yes? The reports? All that comes with the invitation."

"Yes, but—"

"You've got the contract detailing your living quarters, work and pay? We have been very well resourced to make this happen. And those who have already gone have helped set things up quite comfortably."

She is still smiling. Patient. Holding her clipboard. "To put it delicately, if you were eligible to apply in the first place, you really need a new start." She consults her clipboard. "In your case, financially, it seems. You can't come back, but you leave your debts behind as well."

"How do I know that it's all true?" he asks. "That what is over there really is? Over there, I mean."

And that is both the crux of it and his big mistake. Her smile disappears.

"Mr Tims, we at Better World are contracted to provide this service and are scrutinised accordingly. Yes, there have been people with concerns before, but our applicants by and large greatly appreciate the opportunity, rather than insinuate unpleasant things."

"I...I guess I'm just having a hard time believing. Believing it's me, I mean. That got picked," Marty says, because that is also true.

"You did apply, and once vetting is completed, selection from the pool of potentials is random. It has to be someone, Mr Tims." She makes some sort of note on her clipboard.

"Um. Has to be?"

Her smile does not reappear. "A poor choice of words, I'm sure. You are one of the lucky ones."

She makes another note on her clipboard and then puts it across her lap.

"I appreciate your reluctance, Mr Tims. The only assurance I can give you is that we truly believe in what we are doing here at Better World." She tips her head towards the door in the far wall. "But you do have the right to leave, of course."

He thinks of the people in the line. The girl in front of him with her spiky hair and raised eyebrow. The father, his thin face crowded with both anxiety and hope. The cheer from the people going through, like they were on a roller coaster.

The wail of the little girl.

"I'm sorry," he says, and stands.

He heads to the exit. Clipboard lady does not move or speak, so he pulls the door open and steps through.

There is a sudden hum from either side, from above and below. Marty turns to see the woman making one more note on her clipboard, and then there is a flash of teal.

He has one last moment to think.

A Better World for who, exactly?

Unfurl

When the sun bleeds dark
across sand and what was.
When The Pale struts and dances on.
Care. Want what you want.
Hold hard to what slips.

When the night lies. When the last mirror cracks,
tell your knotted side, the tight and roiling red
Wake!
And watch for its eager eyes.

When you swim above the darkness
Kicking. And the many cold hands
pull on your frantic legs.
Give the matted thing inside
its snarling voice.

When Fingermen of the dark emerge
With their disregard. With their blank faces.
As the shards of right fall away
Trembling. You must realise
or remember for the first time
your beast can bite to the end.

The Skin Trader

Auntie grunts as she heaves the last huge pot into place. A few wingnuts need tightening, but otherwise it's ready. She waves one hand in front of her face, trying to get the cloud of midges to give her some breathing space, but they barely react to her slow movements. It's this goddamn skin she is wearing. Thick, horny, mottled. She has skimped on the flexibility again, and it shows. She scowls. She should fix that. Customers, those that really need what she is offering, they don't want their skin to slow them down.

The spot she has found is down by the old river front. The market is huge, selling everything from local delicacies to semi-legal transports both on- and off-world. Strings of fission-powered lights strung between the stalls twinkle against the dark indigo sky, and the air is full of market sounds – yells and calls and odd-canted music. This world boasts three moons, but they are all small, pitiful things. If she ignores them, she could be anywhere. The alleys of the smaller stalls meander almost aimlessly towards the water, and most of the shoppers have long since found what they need before they get close to the marshy shoreline. It suits her. She plugs in the fission battery and then opens the pot. The goo inside is slowly swirling, on the edge of solidifying. She will have to cook it for a while before adding the colours and pumping it out onto the skintex expandable moulds, but she doesn't really care. These ones are just for show, not the money makers.

She looks up as someone stops at the next stall, but she knows it will be days before a real buyer seeks her out. This woman is tall and willowy, wearing a pink and orange skin that is so thin and flexible Auntie can see her muscles and fascia underneath. A nice job, if you go for that sort of thing, but purely cosmetic. The pinkish woman glances at Auntie and then looks quickly away, sniffing delicately. Auntie twists her thick lips up into an open-mouthed, breathy smile. This backwater planet is like a thousand others. The people are uppity, and think they are so smart. And most of them are happy to ignore whatever stupid upheaval is going on. She doesn't remember the details, and she doesn't care. She follows the credits, and she can almost smell them here. She will just have to wait, like usual.

He comes at dusk. Auntie is stirring the goo idly with a broken stick, and watching the indigo sky. She has made some skins, thick, bumpy things, pouring them into moulds and using the auto-stretcher to get them more or less to standard sizes before hanging them out for display. Of course no one wants them. The few who glance her way with what might be recognition in their eyes do not venture close. But like always, word carries, and like always, someone has come.

He wears a completely nondescript grey skin under his black one-suit. His eyes are pale and lifeless. They probably come with the skin, Auntie thinks. He fingers one of the skins.

"Pretty thick," he comments. Auntie says nothing. She knows what will come next. He drops the skin and pretends to look through the others.

"Tough enough to stop a standard fission rifle," he says, not looking at her. It is almost a question. Auntie says nothing, and the man goes back to fingering one of the skins.

"Can you do this mottling in brown and green?" he asks. She nods slowly. She has not got around to re-skinning herself, and her neck feels stiff and thick.

The man looks at her then, expressionless.

"DNA mixes?" he asks quietly.

Auntie cocks her head slightly. His pale eyes flick left and right.

"DNA mixes in skinmaking is illegal," she says.

"Do you do them?" he asks. "Can you?"

Auntie hesitates, looking at his pale eyes. She has learnt to be cautious. Finally she gives an almost imperceptible nod.

"How many?" she asks. It turns out he wants a lot. They always do.

Days later, and one of the little moons has faded to a sliver when the man reappears. Auntie is waiting. She has his skins, not stretched yet, row upon row of them packed into small containers. They are very tough, very thick, mottled how he wants. They are ready for the DNA mix-in, and will take it deep, bleeding the changes throughout the body from where the nano-grafts take hold in the muscle. She is good at that, the best. They will pass all but the most invasive, most difficult checks.

They swoop in from all around. One presses a small firearm to the back of her head, while others start searching her stall. They pull apart her equipment, and one tips over the largest skin pot. Liquid skin bubbles as it flows across the dirt. The man steps forward and opens up the container as Auntie sits very still. It is empty, and he looks up sharply. His eyes are not flat anymore, and his skin is not grey. Both eyes and skin are now dark purple, like the sky, like the mark of the local ruling clan.

"What is this?" he snaps. Auntie sits very still, and with a sound of exasperation the man gestures roughly. A camo-skinned woman steps forward and grabs Auntie under the arm to haul her up. She collapses in a heap at the woman's touch, and the woman yells and jumps back, dropping the flopping, empty skin. There are gasps, confusion, yelling. The man looks around, his anger slowly being replaced by disgust. Such a simple trick, and they have lost her.

Auntie watches from a few stalls away. She has finally gotten around to making herself a new skin. Pinkish orange, and very light, very flexible. She hates it, but she has learnt to be cautious, learnt to blend in. This world is like any other. She picks up her containers and sets off up an alleyway. For the first time she takes more than a passing interest in the people around her. She wonders who has a problem with this ruling clan. She wonders how much of a discount she might just give a genuinely interested party.

Blipcoin

Davos touches the spot behind his ear to set his Memorex chip to record. He will need it both for the interview and his other business. He doesn't try to stop his smirk as the asteroid comes into view. It is a wannabe villain's hideout, hidden amongst the rubble of a wider belt of floating rubble. Davos has seen plenty of places like this. He has interviewed plenty of rebels, dissidents, and self-absorbed tech-heads who just can't handle reality. They all come and go. Often they go right after he is done interviewing them. Not all of them—that would be too obvious. He knows that. So do his contacts in the Amalgam.

Flying without network access isn't easy, but Davos is used to such meet conditions. He docks manually, but the lone guard in the dusty little hangar doesn't look impressed. Davos is ever underappreciated. Underestimated.

Network security seems as non-existent as the physical, and he just can't help himself.

"You don't want to check my chip? I could have a Trojan horse in my head. Shall I just walk on in?" He has been scanned dozens of times. The uplink hidden in his chip, his direct contact to the Amalgam, is undetectable and massively encrypted.

The guard just shrugs and points. Davos shrugs right on back and walks down the indicated tunnel. There are a few people, but not many. No one pays him any attention, and soon enough he is stepping through a door into an irritatingly plain room with rock walls. Dullness does not help sell interviews, even when the subject is an Amalgam outlaw.

Said outlaw is sitting at a bare metal table in the centre of the room. He is younger than Davos expected. Actually, he is not much more than a snot-nosed kid in a rumpled shirt and loose pants. He hasn't combed his hair.

"The famous Davos," the kid grins, toying with a retro-style tablet.

"The infamous X," Davos replies. What kind of name is X, anyway? Still, he tries to keep the snark out of his voice. Selling this interview to a major outlet could net him a decent payday, given the whispers about Blipcoin. And selling the kid's location to the Amalgam will get him enough cash for something like six months on Ferdial 6. Half a year of soaking up the rays of those famous twin suns for real, rather than in a pale Memorex sim.

The kid looks pleased, and Davos struggles not to roll his eyes.

"I was surprised by the invite," he says instead. That is, of course, a lie. Someone like X always wants to tell their story, their side of things, and Davos is the best investigative reporter across ten populated systems. Maybe eleven, after this.

"Tell me about Blipcoin," Davos continues. Yes, he should banter. He should build some trust. But he really just wants to sit on the beach under warm suns and drink exotic cocktails, not be here inside this dirty rock talking to a jumped-up petty criminal.

X waves at an empty chair across the table. “Tell me what you know, first.”

Davos sits down. “It’s an illegal currency. You are trading it across dark-links in the network, and have built quite the following. Quite the customer base.”

The kid looks unimpressed. That is just tabloid gossip, after all. But tech rebels all have two things in common: they think they are smarter than the Amalgam, and they like to brag about it.

“Sounds just like those twenty-first century crypto currencies. I hope your Blipcoin lasts a bit longer than them,” Davos says.

The kid takes the bait. “Oh,” he says, “it is so much more than that.”

Every malcontent thinks they have something special. That they are something special.

“False digital currency is classed as counterfeiting by the Amalgam,” Davos says. “They will lock you away for life.”

“If they catch me,” X replies, and then his smile disappears and he leans forward, his gaze suddenly not so childish. “If you tell them where I am.”

Davos manages to keep his face still, but it’s a struggle. He has always been so careful. It has always just been him, his Memorex chip, and his contacts in the Amalgam.

X smiles again.

“My father was quite the programmer. His little company was very much in demand for fixing bugs in all sorts of systems. He was too good, in the end, too much of a security risk. I don’t know what happened to him. Not yet. The Amalgam keeps those types of records in their private network."

"I don't know what you are talking about," Davos says. "I'm just a reporter."

X picks up the tablet, fiddles with it.

"Over the years, my father built up a phenomenal client base. Fixing code. Fixing glitches. Fixing all those little blips."

"Blips?"

X nods. "Remove a blip. And maybe add a dark-link entry point in the code."

Davos feels his face go pale.

"Blipcoin..."

X taps the tablet. "Blipcoin is not currency. Blipcoin is a key. A key to many things. Including, of course, Memorex. And now, through your uplink, directly to the Amalgam."

The pale tones of a Memorex sim begin to wash across Davos's vision. He feels the warmth of twin tropical suns on his skin, hears the crashing of waves.

"I'm sorry," X says, his voice fading. "I could work on your uplink from anywhere, but I don't think I can let you keep running around working for the Amalgam. I can give you one last little sim visit to Ferdial 6, though."

The Downloaded Detective and the Swollen Technician

Bleeding. I am bleeding out, and someone is standing over me, telling me they are right and I am wrong. That is all I can remember. Nothing else. I have lost everything.

I raise my hand towards my head and see it's metal. My hand, that is. That's enough to trigger my new cyber-synapses or inference engine or whatever I've got in this model. I haven't lost my memory. The transfer is just slow—a trickle.

Suspected wrongful death. That is something that has downloaded.

"Um. Investigator for Sector 22.69? Are you in there?" a voice asks. A young female. Nervous.

Nice deduction, Sector 22.69 Investigator.

I sit up and swing my legs off the table. I'm in some sort of medical area. I can't feel the surface underneath me, but embedded sensors of one type or another in my new body tell me it is smooth and chilly. So I have some semblance of touch, then. That's good. Sight is close to normal, maybe a bit of a lag with tracking but nothing bad. No infrared, which is a shame. Hearing is obviously okay.

"What model am I in?" I ask. My voice is tinny. Something basic, then. A bot they had on hand, which is common.

That's a scrap of situational memory, dribbling in with other stuff. Like the fact that I keep noting in my reports that the speed of download is correlated with success of investigation. Sector Government Office 22.69 doesn't seem to care much about that, though.

"An Umwelt Assist Five with Preparatory Enhancement."

I swivel my head towards the voice. Movement response standard. Good. Good all round, really. When you have nothing, you appreciate the little things.

The woman is indeed young. She is also so squared away in her security uniform it would hurt my eyes if I had nerve endings. Grey pants, grey shirt, both as wrinkle free as my new metal face (presumably), with a thin piping of white on the pants seam. She has a little cap on, and epaulets with two white stripes. She also has a sleek black side-arm on her hip—some sort of pulse weapon. Her face is narrow and she is biting her lip as she regards me with big eyes.

The bot-bound usually freak people out.

"Your name?" I ask.

"Talia," she says. "Security Officer Talia Jenkins."

"Give me a moment, Security Officer Jenkins," I say, and stand myself up. Pretty decent balance. No vertigo. Transfer has been seamless. I take a couple of steps and then do a squat. Nice. A little stiff, but no issues. Except... I bring my other hand up to my face. Or would, except it's not a hand. My arm ends with a fat canister sporting a flexible nozzle.

"What's this?" I ask her.

"It's a surfactant pack," she says. "The Preparatory Enhancement of the Umwelt is usually for cargo bay prep."

"I grease the tracks?" I ask. I want to laugh, but a dead person laughing inside a bot upsets people.

"I suppose so," she says. "Sorry, there wasn't much choice. There is a med-bot, but it was busy."

Oh well. Neuron-mapped dead individuals who bounce between star systems can't be picky. I'll take what I can get.

"Okay then, Officer Jenkins," I say. "Let's see this dead body."

I've been dead for two years, but I've been a Sector Investigator for ten. That's a piece of information that downloads pretty quickly each time—right after the details about bleeding out. Nice and depressing, but I guess remembering it early has its uses. It's grounding. Also, good for boundaries. Recalling my own situation makes me extra-reluctant to talk about being bot-bound with people like Security Officer Jenkins. Not talking about death and mortality is a good boundary to have with new acquaintances.

There is no real reason to download me in a medical area, but that is usually what happens. For some reason people equate it with a medical procedure, even though it is more like updating your comms system, or getting a new media file. A really big one. In this case being in medical is useful, as the dead body is apparently next door.

The short walk across the infirmary confirms my current body is fine, except I do find myself glancing at my spray-can hand. Weird, even for me. I hope this investigation does not require anything with a high degree of dexterity.

The door slides open and I follow Jenkins into the pseudo-surgical area. It's tiny, which is standard for long-haul, low-staffed ships. The first person we meet is the Captain, who is wearing the same uniform as Jenkins except he has four white stripes on his epaulets and his hat is bigger.

"Jenkins, what took so long?" he snaps. He does not appear to be taking the situation in stride. Jenkins starts to say something, but I hold up one hand. My spray-can hand. I swap it for the other.

"The download can take some time," I say. "I am the Sector Investigator."

He gives me an almost startled look, which tells me he hasn't had to deal with a bot-bound before. We aren't exactly common, or cheap to create, but beaming one of us in is cheaper than putting a specialist on every ship in case of a rare event like murder.

Hopefully a rare event.

"Who died?" I ask. I've still got nothing more than that *suspected wrongful death* bouncing around in my head. Maybe it's download lag but it probably means there is nothing else. The Sector Office has this annoying thing about empty slates and starting with them.

"Technician Joss Blare, Maintenance."

The speaker is a short woman in a grey uniform much like Jenkins' and the Captain. She has just come around a kind of semi-rigid curtain that has been set up in the middle of the room. Her face is lined and her hair is shot through with grey. Over her uniform she is wearing a disposable green apron and long gloves, both smeared with shocks of bright scarlet, and she has just removed a serious combination mask and breathing unit.

"Investigator," she says. "I am Doctor Eziel."

"Call me Alex," I say, even though no one ever does. It is better than Investigator or Umwelt Assist or tin-man. And it was my name once.

Bleeding out. I am bleeding out.

"What's with the blood?" I ask. I hope it's not an old-style murder with a sociopath running around the ship. That would be okay to solve, because sociopaths and the like are easy to pick out in a limited crowd. But they often start thinning the herd before you can nail them down, and that isn't great for my final report, or the herd.

She touches the curtain and it concertinas back into itself. There is a white table identical to the one I just woke up on. This one also has someone dead on it, but in a different way. He won't be walking around playing detective any time soon.

A med-bot is standing by the table, in the act of using its delicate pincer-like digits to stitch Technician Joss Blare's chest up. There is still a fair bit more than usual on display. I catch the sound of hurried movement behind me, and then the Captain being sick somewhere nearby.

I step forward and bend to inspect the dead man's face. He is young, and nondescript, but he is also...puffy. His lips are thickened and slightly split, and his eyes bulge.

"Why is there a doctor on board?" I ask, without turning around. Usually there is a med-bot, or perhaps just one of the human crew with some training on med equipment if whatever haulage company under contract is really skimping.

"I'm with the Mollusc Biologist," she says, a bit frostily. People don't like being asked why they are around during a murder investigation, particularly those who are used to their own authority.

"And why does the Mollusc Biologist need a doctor?" I ask. I turn around, and she is regarding me without a smile.

"I have training in Xeno-anatomy and physiology," Eziel says.

"And?" I prompt.

"They are doing Mollusc physiology research," the Captain says. He has recovered from his temporary illness, although he is pale and won't look at the table. "It's all approved."

"Okay," I say. By "they", I'm guessing the doc and the on-board Mollusc Biologist. Grav-slugs are always being researched, since they are critical for interstellar travel and also extremely bizarre lifeforms. And that is coming from a guy who died years ago and is currently piloting a bot with one hand geared up for quick application of lubricant.

Maybe I'll ask the doc more about her slug fascination later, but right now I've got a dead body to get back to.

"Why cut him open?" I ask. "You've got scans."

I can say that because they are currently displayed on a big screen next to the med-bot. I step closer and read the summary. Widespread organ damage. Liver bloat. Heart leakage. Blood flow irregularities.

Brain swelling.

"I needed to double check those," Eziel says. I get that. The technician is a mess. It would have been easier to believe the med-bot was defective.

“I also wanted to take cultures from the organs. I could have had the med-bot do it with pinhole intrusions, but again—”

“You wanted to be sure.” That makes sense as well.

“Nothing infectious,” she says. “In case you were worried.”

I had been. And still was, just not about infection.

“But the med-bot was right,” she keeps on. “His organs are full of micro-tears. And the limbs, stretched and torn at all the joints.” She touches the dead man’s arm, and then his head. “This is the worst. It’s a mess in there.”

A tough way to go—tougher than being shot several times by a bot trafficker who glared down at me as I bled.

I’m going to change it all, he had said. *I’m going to change my life*.

Everyone wants change. It’s the real killer.

The trafficker had started to say more, and that was when a Security Officer a few years older than Jenkins had shot him. Then he’d been lying next to me, and all I could see as I was dying was the fury in his eyes.

Of course that memory downloads with no problem.

The Captain speaks up from behind us.

“So what killed him?”

Eziel shakes her head, but I know the look in her eyes. I’ve seen my share of barely contained fear. It crops up a lot out in deep space, when people are surrounded by a few bots and a lot of nothing.

“I don’t know,” she says. “But it would’ve hurt like nothing I can imagine.”

Jenkins' office is too clean. I am seated because it disturbs people when a dead person stands around tirelessly in a bot's body, and she is sitting behind her desk, staring at me.

We have just visited the small, dead-end corridor where Blare was found. There was nothing but a spill of precision tools on the floor near an open access panel, and I had asked to retreat to somewhere quiet. I'd needed to go over what I knew, which had not taken long.

"What's it like?" she asks. I know what she is asking about. Someone always does.

I go for a shrug but my shoulders are fixed in place.

"It's like sleeping," I say. It's not, but that will do. "You rest, then you are awake, like now. Then you are working. Sometimes I load into a sim. Like a holiday."

"But that sounds terrible," she says. I doubt she is the murderer, if murder it has been. She is too honest.

"Yes," I say, not pointing out that she does just about the same. And it's not as terrible as being shot six times and left to bleed out on the floor of some grubby Lunar Station by someone who spits on you while you are dying.

"I take what I can get," I say. I say that a lot—mostly to myself. "It was opt-in in my original employment contract. Came with a bonus. Transfer at point of death if feasible."

I had signed with no thought. It is so rarely feasible.

"Are you okay with it?" she asks.

"Yes," I reply. Which is not true, but also is. Who is happy with their life? But I guess right now I'm more alive than not, and for a longer stretch than I should have gotten.

Stretch. Huh.

"He was swollen," I say. "The technician. His lips. His face."

The Umwelt has very limited access to the ship's systems, so I've had to go back to manual retrieval. I've brought up Blare's records on a handheld, and his staff photo confirms. He was much puffier than he should have been.

"What would make every limb, every muscle, every organ stretch?" I muse.

She shakes her head, now a little pale.

"Okay," I keep on, slowly. Got to test the logic. Theories have to be solid when you are floating in deep space with a dead body. "What if the opposite had happened?"

Jenkins frowns. "Like everything pressed together?"

"Yes. What would cause that?"

"Then I'd say he had been crushed. Just a bit, if you can say that—crushed just a bit." She chews on her lip. "Acceleration, maybe?" she says.

"An increase in gravity?" I counter, even though it's the same thing.

Her eyes widen. There is only one place on the ship that screws around with gravity.

Time to visit the slug.

Every ship has the same basic setup: a big ring that turns, and a spindle in the middle for the ring to turn around. Most of the spindle is a huge bundle of motors and bearings that keep the ring moving, and some complicated stuff that lets the spindle turn as well. Right at the centre of all those moving parts is the Habitat. This one is a little bigger than most, because this ship has a lot of cargo space, but it's standard otherwise. We enter the space from the bottom, using the closest entrance to

Jenkins' office, a service ladder. That is a mistake, as it turns out it's extremely hard to climb a ladder with a spray-can hand.

I manage it in the end, and we emerge into the Habitat. There is a control panel in the centre of the room, and a transparent wall that partitions off a big chunk of the space.

"What are you doing in here?"

I turn to see a good-looking woman in a pair of work overalls holding a handheld. I'd looked her up before we left Jenkins' office, so I know who she is.

"Dr Miren," I say.

She walks to the control panel and slides her handheld into a slot.

"What do you want?" she asks.

"I want to find out what happened to Technician Blare," I say. "But I'll take some common courtesy to start with."

"You have no business in here," she says. Her gaze is flat. "Check the logs if you want. I was in here when Blare was found, and well before that too."

I'd like to say she just hates the bot-bound, but it's likely she has never even met one. She probably just doesn't like being questioned for murder. Funny how people react to that.

Beyond the transparent wall is the Habitat proper. The floor in there is rough, dry gravel, and here and there larger rocks are crowded together. There are some low purplish shrubs with oddly ethereal branches and leaves that seem to float. The ambient light in there is a nice, soothing dusk.

"Where's the slug?" I ask. It's what I came to ask about, after all.

"She's not a slug," the doctor says. I don't reply, and after a second she points off to the left.

"She was using a gravity well to bend the light," she says in an odd mix of accusation and pride. "She doesn't like strangers."

The thing is slowly becoming visible, shimmering and blurring around the edges still, but coming into focus. It's big for an Inertial Mollusc, taller and longer than a person, with lurid yellow stripes down its back and three jelly-filled eyes waving around on long stalks. I haven't seen this type before, or if I have, good old Sector Office hasn't bothered reminding me. There are variants of them on several extremely high-grav worlds, huge and boneless and bizarre. But they all have two things in common: they eat gravitons, and they are almost solely responsible for successful interstellar travel. They do weird things with gravity, which means they do weird things to space and distance. The spinning Habitat can be regulated via g-forces to produce more or less gravitons for the beast, and there is some complicated machinery in the walls that use the localised change in particles to amplify and channel effects. In essence, the slugs are a spark to a flame, the flame being interstellar warping of space.

I don't understand much more than that. I'm a dead investigator made up of neuron-mapping code and fragmented governmental download packages of memory, not an expert in quantum gravity and extra-terrestrial zoology. Not a Mollusc Biologist, in other words.

I step closer to the wall and all three of the slug's large, saucer-like eyes swivel in my direction. The yellow stripes down its back start to pulse.

"You are scaring her," Dr Miren says.

"Do they have a defence mechanism?" I ask. The yellow pulsing speeds up and the back half of the slug disappears.

"They have the localised gravity well, what Evelyn is doing now. That's bending light," Miren says. She is trying for casual now but there is definitely pride in her voice. And affection.

Evelyn. The slug is named Evelyn.

"Anything else?" Miren asks. She wants me gone.

So much for the soft approach.

"Perhaps," I say. "You're an expert on gravity. What would kill someone by pulling them apart from the inside? Swollen brain, torn organs like they are overfilled balloons, stretched out arms and legs?"

If I was less of a professional I would be satisfied by the sudden draining of colour from Miren's face. She looks past me at the slug.

"It's not her."

I say nothing.

"Check the logs!" she says. Almost shouts. "Check the Habitat schematics! She can't get out! And if she were wandering around feeding off loose gravitons, the ship would drop into an uncontained space-time distillation, or the gravity fluctuations would tear it apart."

Tear it apart. Just like Technician Joss Blare, Maintenance.

We are back in the security office. Jenkins has stopped looking at me with those big, half-spooked eyes. She doesn't want to say we are stuck. I don't want to say I'm stuck. My job performance is all I have, unless things change for me. And there is really only one change now.

“Well,” Jenkins says, her voice even. “There are no discrepancies in the logs. Not that we are sure the ship could detect a mollusc.” She pauses for a moment before continuing. “But I think the doctor is right. That thing is huge. If it got out and started feeding, we’d all be floating in space surrounded by nothing more than shards of metal. Or in one of those space-time distilled things.”

She’s right. I’ve also gone through the logs. Same conclusion. Evelyn went nowhere and did nothing.

I go back to the handheld and flick over to the medical report on Blare. Well, I try to. Stupid spray-can hand. I swap hands and get the report up. Liver damage. Limbs stretched. Blood vessels leaking.

Brain swollen.

Eziel touching his head.

This is the worst.

“Talia,” I say, “the corridor where Blare was found. It went nowhere, right?”

“Yes,” she says. “A nub passage connecting to one of the spindle ruts. Nothing out of the ordinary.”

“There was an access panel, but I think also a vent just down the corridor. Are there pipes in there? Ducting of some sort?”

Talia pulls out her handheld and taps away. After a moment she nods.

“There is ducting, but it’s small. Maybe a hand-width wide. It looks like it’s for access to rotation control fibres.”

“At head height, if I recall?”

Talia squints and then looks up, puzzled. “Just about, yes. But that duct is way too small for anyone or anything. I mean, that slug couldn't get through there. They might be boneless, but there is still the mass to volume ratio issue."

"You're right," I say. "She couldn't."

It's just a hunch, but it feels right. I stand up.

"Let's go," I say.

The first thing I see when we climb back into the Habitat control room is Eziel. She is breathing heavily through her nose, obviously upset. Miren is standing in front of her, her gaze hard.

"What's going on?" I ask.

I get silence, so I focus on Eziel.

"Doctor Eziel, what are you doing here?"

"That's none of your business," she snaps.

"Actually, it is. I'm in the middle of a wrongful death investigation, and right now, I'm thinking you're a person of interest." I flick my gaze towards Miren. "Both of you."

"I'm the ship's doctor!" Eziel exclaims.

"And I'm the Government Investigator for this Sector. The moment I downloaded, this ship came under my full jurisdiction." I pause. "But you can just be arrested, if you prefer."

"For what?"

"Hindering an official investigation. Maybe murder."

Eziel snorts.

"Security Officer Jenkins," I say, "take Doctor Eziel to her quarters for confinement. Then inform the Captain."

Talia steps forward and Eziel's eyes widen.

"Wait!" she says. "It wasn't me."

"Stop."

It's Miren. She is staring at me. Her eyes are still dark with fury. I've seen that look before. It's the look of someone cornered, exposed, but defiant. The look of someone who believes they are justified in their actions.

It is the look of a bot trafficker standing over a bleeding Investigator who forgot to clear the room properly.

I go to hold up one hand—spray-can again, damn it. I swap hands, and Talia pauses.

"Tell me," I say to the Mollusc Biologist. I think I've gotten a fair bit of it right, although Eziel was a surprise.

"It's not Mariah's fault," she says, looking from me to Eziel. "I needed some help, and she thought we were just doing a physiology study when she signed on."

"Help with what, exactly?"

She stares at me, still defiant.

I feel the bullets. I see those eyes, looking down at me as I lay on the floor two years and a lifetime ago.

"Help with delivering Evelyn's baby."

I had guessed it. A wild, crazy guess born from the size of the duct and poor Blare's swollen head.

Talia speaks, her disbelief plain.

"The Inertial Mollusc was pregnant? It gave birth on the ship, in the Habitat? That is against every regulation!"

"Only because we don't know anything about their gestation and mothering in captivity, and how are we ever going to find out if we don't study it?" Miren retorts.

Poor Blare. Stretched to pieces for the sake of Miren's obsession.

"Right now," I say, "I'm more interested in where the thing is."

At that, Eziel pipes up.

"That's what we were talking about. I came to tell Dr Miren she should tell you what had happened. That we need to find the baby." She shrugs. "Now you know."

"So, this baby slug? Slugette? Whatever—it's not in Habitat?" I ask.

Miren shakes her head.

"Let me guess," I continue. "It went out through the ducts and hasn't come back?"

She nods. She has the grace to look chagrined. Slightly.

"But if we get it back, the fact we have been successful, birthed a slug, we have so much data," she says. "It would be the biggest breakthrough. No more wild catching efforts! Breeding programs. Expansion! No limit to travel. The benefits are huge!"

"I guess that 'we' you mention doesn't include Technician Blare?" I ask.

"None of that matters," Eziel says. "We need to get it back before it does something to the ship. Or anybody else."

A long silence follows, and then Talia speaks.

"It eats gravitons, right? So why don't we feed it?"

Miren stares at her like she is a piece of furniture that just had a good idea, and then nods. "Yes. I can do that. If I ramp up the spin on the Habitat, the relative centrifugal force will throw out more gravitons. Evelyn will get most of them, but there might be enough to lure the baby back in."

She doesn't wait for a response but turns to the control panel and starts punching at the screen. If there is a change in the rotation of the room that the others notice, it is not something the Umwelt Assist picks up on. Evelyn is another matter. She is well back from the wall, swaying a little, turned partly away. The yellow stripes up her back are pulsing slowly, rhythmically.

"She's feeding," Miren says quietly, almost reverently. "It will make her groggy, kind of dopey."

We stand in silence. Nothing happens. Miren, at the control panel, starts to look worried, and Eziel is fidgeting.

"How safe are these things?" Talia asks abruptly. "I mean, did Blare do anything other than be in the wrong place at the wrong time? Did the baby attack him out of self-defence, or was it hungry or panicked or something?"

Oh, no.

I turn to Miren.

"It will come back in through the duct it went out of." She gestures towards the far wall of the Habitat, beyond Evelyn. But she doesn't look at me, or Talia.

"And is that the only duct in this room?" I ask.

Too late. I am too late. Maybe she has done it on purpose. Maybe not, but I have made a mistake regardless. Just like when I walked into a dimly-lit room on a Lunar Station thinking too much about my investigation and not enough about anything else until the bullets tore through me.

Eziel screams.

I spin around. She has retreated back towards the access ladder. I can't see a vent, and it doesn't matter now.

The doctor is still screaming as I move. Something so bizarre is happening I wonder if there is something wrong with the bot's visual processors. The wrinkles on her face start to smooth out. It only takes a moment until her skin is fresh and taut. Then it keeps going. Her eyes start to bug out just like Blare's. She opens her mouth to scream again and her swollen lips split, spraying blood.

I'm almost on her.

"There!" Talia yells, "On top of her head!"

First there is nothing, and then a slight shimmer in the air. It's a gravity well. The thing is perched on top of Eziel's head, bending light around itself.

I reach out, not sure what I'm going to do, and Eziel stops screaming. Her bulging eyes roll, and then she falls. Her head hits the ground with a sound that is too wet.

Maybe because it is young, or not practiced, or panicked, the baby slug drops its camouflage as it hits the floor and slides. It is translucent blue, with dual yellow stripes running up its back. Three tiny eyes on stalks wave wildly. Dimly I hear the sound of a door sliding open.

It's the Habitat door. Miren is at the control panel. She is snarling in her righteousness. We are in the way of change. In the way of her progress.

"No!" I shout. It comes out in a tinny warble.

Talia has her pulse weapon out and is pointing it at the baby slug, but is distracted by my attempted shout. She turns her head and stares as Evelyn slides towards the open door. The mother slug is not going fast, though—I guess she is still dopey from her feeding.

Dr Miren plows into Talia from the back, and the Security Officer stumbles. Her weapon goes off as she falls and my arm jerks backward. I look down to find my one useful hand has become a shattered mess.

Miren kicks the weapon away and then bends down.

"Come here, baby," she croons. She is all dark eyes and intense focus now, as if we don't exist, as if we suddenly are no threat. Miren is selfish, yes. Righteous as well. Delusional? Most definitely. "It will be okay," she says.

The slugette doesn't hesitate. It goes straight to her and up her outstretched arms. I have enough time to think that it knows her and she is not completely crazy, and then it reaches her shoulder and she starts screaming.

Evelyn is halfway to her door.

Talia is winded but climbing to her feet. I am quicker. I stride forward and reach out as Miren stands upright, her face slack with shock and pain.

"Help me!" she screams into my borrowed face.

I go to grab the thing from her, and for once I use my correct hand, which is now useless. I prod the thing with my shattered fingers and it jerks back from me as Miren staggers to the side.

One hand, now down to no hands. Just a spray can.

What the hell.

I point my nozzle at the Mollusc Biologist and her passenger and give them a dose of cargo bay surfactant. Apparently something down there in haulage needed a lot of lubricating, because the nozzle ejects a huge cloud of whitish mist that envelops the overconfident doctor and the slugette.

Miren screams again, and raises one hand to her face. Her other hand, on the side of the slug, just flops there—*stretched.*

The baby slug's reaction is just as immediate. It shivers and tries to curl up into itself. Then it emits a tiny, desperate mewling and drops to the floor with a splat. It slithers away, fast, and before I can say or do anything, Talia kicks it towards the open Habitat door.

The thing rolls over and over and then slides itself the last few feet to the threshold. Evelyn is there, and I have one moment where I think she will come out and we will all be stretched apart but the baby slides inside and then Talia is at the control panel. She scans it frantically and then slaps at something.

The door closes. There is more mewling from the other side of the wall, but I don't look. I don't want anything else to do with the damn slugs.

"Are you okay?" I ask Talia. She is obviously shaken but nods. Then she trains her side arm on the Mollusc Biologist.

Miren is kneeling on the floor. She is grasping her damaged arm with her one working hand. At least she still has one working hand, in a mostly working body. Her eyes are red and her face looks shiny, but she can see.

She is not even looking at me or Talia. She is staring at the Habitat. At Evelyn, and the baby.

"They will still change everything," she says.

I'm going to change it all.

I could say a lot to that. I could tell her she is deluded, and a murderer. I could tell her that her idea of change got people killed. I could tell her change comes for us all, so there is no need to rush it.

Maybe I even believe that.
Maybe.

Stutter

Evan cuts between the lab and the cabling that runs to the ion generator. He's not supposed to, but it's not like it matters if he knocks the surge protector again. Besides, he wants to get Catherine her coffee while he is still himself, and this is the quickest way from the kitchenette.

He has also made her a sandwich.

He is just through the door of the computation lab when the world begins to shift. Sometimes it is lightning fast, sometimes it stretches out. He manages to set both the mug and the sandwich on the edge of the desk as the air seems to bunch and tense.

Catherine feels it, of course. Evan is the centre of the storm, but ripping reality apart is not something that is subtle. She smiles at him. There is only a little sadness there. They haven't known each other very long, but they have also known each other for years.

She points at one of the computer screens with one hand and pushes her too-long fringe back with the other.

"Not much progress I'm afr—" and then the room flexes and she is gone.

Except that is just how it seems to Evan. He is the one who was in the ion station when the power spiked. He is the unstable one. So while to him he is always him, he is really just bouncing around now.

A quantum stutter.

Yet from his viewpoint, she is the one who has changed. Now she is a Catherine with a smattering of freckles and glasses. Also, her hair is blonde.

"Damn it," this Catherine scowls at him, and then turns back to the computer.

"Dr Michaels," she says curtly. "I hope you are more competent than your predecessor."

This Catherine takes her coffee with two sugars and milk. So far that's very much in the minority.

She does say "thank you" when he puts the mug down next to her, but doesn't look away from the screen.

"What do you think?" she asks without looking around. "Should we invert this vector here?"

He doesn't say anything. She starts typing.

"You are supposed to know more about ion-induced quantum states than anyone," she says. "We don't have much more time before someone notices."

She's right, he supposes. They have a lot of autonomy, but it won't be long before questions are asked.

"Dr Jamieson," he starts. She doesn't look at him.

"Catherine," he tries.

"Huh?" She glances at him. She has that little furrow between her eyes that he knows so well. It hurts to see it.

"Here," he says, holding out the plate with the sandwich. He had to remake it after the stutter, but that's okay. He's made quite a few sandwiches over the last couple of days.

"You should eat. It's tuna with mayonnaise and capers."

The little furrow deepens.

"That's my favourite," she says.

"I figured," he says. "It was my Catherine's favourite too."

Then the world stutters again.

This one is fast. He stumbles and grabs at the desk to steady himself. He knocks a mug of coffee to the floor, and the now black liquid splatters up one leg of Catherine's jeans.

This Catherine has dark hair in a bob, like she mostly does, but she is wearing a t-shirt. Some heavy metal band thing. That's new.

She sighs and gives him a smile that is only an echo of what he wants. So far, it's as close as he has come.

"Hello, Evan. Yet again."

At least he is Evan here, not Dr Michaels. This Catherine has been scribbling on a notepad rather than using the computer. She holds it up.

"What do you think?" she says, pointing at the equations. "Any closer?"

It's not.

The world stutters, and he is gone.

“Evan, check this. Is it right, do you think?” the next Catherine asks. Her eyes are red and her face is drawn. He wonders if this version of her has taken any break at all since the accident.

She is pointing at a screen that is full of integrals and phase shift iterations. One glance is enough for him. She has made a very obvious mistake.

“I don’t know,” he says.

“Yes, you do,” she says. “I think we need to talk.”

She’s frowning, and he can see that little furrow between her eyes.

“How about I get us a coffee first?” Evan tries. “And something to eat. A sandwich?”

Catherine smiles. It looks pained.

“Tuna and capers?” she asks, and then rubs at her face. “My Evan liked to make me that. It’s my favourite. His, too.”

Her Evan. Like his Catherine.

“But no,” she says, and points at the error on the screen. “Most Evans help. Some don’t. You’re one of those. Tell me why.”

He waits for a stutter. Nothing happens, and even though she is not his Catherine, he can’t stand the lack of trust in her eyes.

There is still a notepad on the desk. He pulls it towards him, starts writing. When he is done he turns it so she can see the equations.

“Oh,” she says softly.

“Yes,” he says. “We can stop it, but we can’t reverse it.”

Some Catherines wouldn’t care. Those that call him Dr Michaels wouldn’t.

But this Catherine has her own Evan.

She is silent for a long time. Evan thinks she is probably working through the odds of her Evan stuttering back to her.

He knows those odds. He has calculated them over and over.

They don't matter.

"Well," she says finally. She smiles—it is resigned, but tinged with something else. Something it took him a lot of stutters to get to.

Hope.

"Maybe we should both have a sandwich," she says. "While we wait."

He feels the same smile on his own face. The odds are long, but that is what he has now. What they both have.

And the world stutters again.

Samantha's Encounter with the Giant Hare in the Valley of Unbreakable Vows, and what came of It

The Valley of Unbreakable Vows has a sign, which Sam stops to check out. Not because the Valley is a surprise or anything (although finding it is a relief), but who does the signage? A local who likes to hike and has some cool woodworking skills? Someone who has vowed to delineate entrances to fabled and dangerous locations?

Maybe the legendary Hare of Vows does the signage, but it would need hands. People seem a bit divided on that point. In one story the Hare claps when someone makes a vow, and it would be pretty hard to do that without hands. But Pamela told her the Hare just smiles at you with its freaky mouth and then hops away.

The sign is not a professional thing, but it's nice. It's wood, with the letters stained or maybe burnt in so the words are dark, close to black. Solid work, but a bit clumsy – the board is mounted on a thick plank surrounded at its base by a bunch of rocks. The whole thing is a little canted, leaning away from the narrow, gravelly path and towards one of the steep canyon walls.

Creepy. Not that anyone would turn back now.

Sam hefts her backpack and eyes the narrow canyon trail. She's been on it for over a day, and she is thirsty and tired because the trail was not wide enough to pitch her little tent so she had slept outside and been bitten by a thousand mosquitos. The rocky walls on either side go up and up and if she stares upwards too much it is like they are merging together overhead, reaching towards each other and squeezing the air into nothing as they whisper at her—*go straight* and *keep on* and *no choice*. A vow before any vow, a practice vow that has shunted her into some dream of step after step and no room to go left or right until she wants to scream, but the canyon walls are finally, finally dropping away just ahead, and there are trees and the sound of water running and even the sun looks a bit brighter.

She scratches at the bites on her arms as she heads on past the sign, and pretends to not be so relieved about leaving that narrow canyon behind. She starts to wonder what is about to happen.

And why she has bothered. There is that to think about, too.

The answer to the first question—what is about to happen—is nothing. Sam walks on out of the narrow canyon, out from that one narrow path and into sunlight that should be pleasant but feels... dull. Weak.

The Valley is pretty, surface-wise. The trees are tall and growing mostly in clusters like they are trying to remember how to be a forest, but there are gaps between them where grey rocks poke up, lichen and moss-covered things like fingers jutting out of the earth. There are swards of grass taking advantage of the thin sun and the larger open spaces. The Valley slopes gently away, and Sam can spy a thin curve of water in the distance, but not too far. A stream rather than a river. The Valley is not as big as she thought it would be, and beyond the stream she can see a mess of rock faces like the canyon behind her and more gentle hillocks that would be an easy walk up and over. She could probably cross the Valley in the morning and not break much of a sweat.

But the sky up above those gentle little hills doesn't look right, and it is kind of like the sunshine. Too pale, too empty. Too flat—washed out paint rather than air or real space that actually goes anywhere. The Valley feels like it is sitting on the edge of things, that she has walked down through that canyon, her life narrowing down until she is here, a pocket that goes nowhere, tells her nothing. A box.

The trail she is standing on widens out and splits into four just before the trees. One snakes left and tracks along the rocky side of the Valley she has just emerged from. The other three slip under the canopy of the nearest tree cluster and out the other side to then make more choices, splitting and splitting again and then each running off away from the others like a net, like coin-tosses over and over, like an ever-growing gaggle of children playing hide and seek.

Sam sits down to work one of her hiking boots off. She has a pebble inside it, or perhaps a blister. She is as new to hiking as the boots are and isn't sure what the problem is, but it's a good time to stop anyway, before she has to pick a path. Her gaze follows one of the gravelly tracks. Switches to another. So many choices out in the Valley, amongst the trees and rocks and grass.

She stares up at that faded sky, those low hillocks. Choices in a box. Choices in front of a painted backdrop.

She slides her pack off and sighs in relief. It's new too, of course, and only really heavy after a few hours of carrying it. She has enough food for another two days if she is careful, plus some water. The Valley is never far, everyone knows that. It's just picky.

Sam finds a tiny grey pebble in her boot and throws it away. She starts to squirm her foot back into the sweaty hole when a voice calls out.

"Hello? Have you made a vow yet? Or are you new?"

She looks around. The voice is low and raspy but clear. She can't see anyone. Maybe it's the Hare. Maybe it's like... the magical voice of the Valley, or something.

"I'm new," she says. It's not like she is going to run and hide from someone or something she can't even see. Also, it doesn't really matter. Things not mattering is why she is here, after all.

Then she sees him—there is a man standing underneath a tree not far away. He is partly in shadow, but mostly she didn't notice him because he is so still. He is dressed in a shabby brown shirt and trousers and he just kind of seems like he is part of everything.

He steps forward, old and thin, and with a scraggly beard and no shoes. His eyes are very pale, leached by time or the intensity of his gaze.

"Can you be my bait then?" he asks.

The man maybe knows what he looks like or sounds like, because he doesn't come any closer. Sam puts her boot back on carefully and stands up. She leaves her pack on the ground, in case she needs to run.

"I'm not dangerous," the man offers, which is not exactly convincing.

"Well," he adds. "Maybe I am, but not to you."

Also not super helpful.

"I'm John," he says.

"Samantha. Sam," Sam says.

"Do you have any food?" he asks, his eyes dropping to her pack.

She bends down and rummages for a muesli bar. When she produces it John snatches it, tears it open, jams the whole thing in his mouth. He starts chewing kind of desperately, his eyes watering. Then he starts coughing.

"Are you okay?" Sam asks.

John coughs again, chews, swallows. He's about to say something, maybe even thank you, then jerks his head up and to one side. His eyes widen as he stares off between the trees.

"Damn!" he says, his voice extra raspy after his coughing. "I'm not ready. Don't make a vow! Please!"

Before Sam can ask what the hell he is on about there is a sound—a breaking branch, a rustling of grass, something moving. She looks to where John had looked. Nothing. Then when she turns back he is gone like he has melted into the ground.

More sounds, and this time when she looks in that direction she sees it slipping out between a couple of trees like there was enough cover for it to have been hidden back there, which there really wasn't.

The Giant Hare of the Valley of Unspeakable Vows.

She doesn't know exactly what she expected, but not this. Sam screams.

Sam doesn't talk to Jerry at work. He's too quiet and too pleasant both, and he is not her immediate supervisor anyway. But he is the one who finds her in the stationery cupboard, which is really a storage closet that sheds any attempt made to change its name, a space that is stalwart and indifferent to usage and semantics and even the occasional, blank-eyed data-entry specialist.

Sam likes the stationery cupboard and hates it as well. Stationery. Stationary. It's like stepping out of time—dark and quiet and there is nothing but staples and post-it notes and pencils, tiny pieces of the larger world that mean nothing without a hand to touch them, to move them, to give them a role. It's like there is nothing beyond the thin walls. A little dark cube, a box. She is in it and away from everything and nothing exists, and that is why she loves it and hates it and can't stop wanting it.

The door opens behind her, letting a wedge of light into the dim space. She should pretend to be doing something—looking for some white-out or some paperclips – but she doesn't bother. She just stands there, mourning the retreating dimness.

Jerry doesn't say anything straight away. He just stands in the doorway like some sort of bespectacled, pale work totem, his thinning hair trying vainly to stop the outside fluorescents reflecting off his scalp.

Finally, he sighs and steps inside. He doesn't close the door. This is work and Human Resources would not be happy about such a thing.

"Samantha," he says. "How many times a week do you hide in here?"

"I'm not," she says. "I'm just... pausing." That's true, but also not. She should feel embarrassed, or angry, or concerned at Jerry's question, but it's too hard. Also, he is smiling his small, thin lipped smile and is as calm as he usually is.

"Is that what you want?" he asks. "To be on pause?"

God, his hair is wispy. The strands of it float like they are trying to escape to a better life. A better head, probably. But Jerry doesn't seem to care. He really doesn't seem like the sort to ever... pause... in the stationary cupboard.

"Are you happy?" she asks. She doesn't mean to, it just kind of pops out.

"Ah," Jerry replies, and the just looks at her for a long time. He isn't smiling, and the light off his scalp doesn't seem silly now. It's just background, and Sam realizes that is what it is about Jerry. He's not background, but he's not foreground either. He's just himself, whatever that is.

Samantha is about to just go, find Martha, her actual supervisor, and maybe cry-off for the day. She could say she had a headache or something. Maybe she could just say it straight out, that the walls of the world around her are too close, too much, too little.

Jerry is pushing up his shirt sleeve. His thin bicep is white even in the poor light, and the tattoo of the Hare is an obvious dark silhouette.

"That's not for me," she says. She has no vow she wants to make.

"You never know," he says.

The Hare winces at Sam's scream and then smiles. The smile is like a gut-punch, and Sam's scream dwindles into a wheeze. Anything this creepy, this uncanny (uncanny in the Valley, *ha ha*), is too big for something like a scream. Just... too much.

The Hare is not really a hare. The thing has the body of a hare, massively overgrown and perhaps six feet tall when sitting, which it is doing now. Its fur is brown peppered through with grey, like it is on the verge of getting old enough to be distinguished. It doesn't have any long ears though and its face is a human face, a smooth, unblemished pink, with small, slightly bulging eyes and thick lips, a moon-round face surrounded by brown and grey fur like a nub of a person is just peering out. A massively oversized, ugly baby face, except its smiles shows perfect white teeth—adult teeth, square and neat and too big.

She stares at it, and it stares at her. Then it sits back a little on its thick hind legs, its hare legs, and it folds its hands together on top of its round bulge of a belly where the fur is a lighter brown.

Yes, hands. Long, fine fingers, and pink like its face. Its wrists are pink and bare too, but the fur comes in halfway up its forearms, fine and wispy but thickening quickly, complete animal fur by the elbows. Sam can't recall if hares have elbows, proper elbows, but this Hare does.

"Hello?" Sam tries. It comes out as a breathy whisper.

The Hare smiles wider. That's all. Sam can't decide whether to look at its face or those long fingered, too-pink hands.

"Hello," Sam tries again, a little louder. The Hare does nothing, says nothing. The silence goes on, with a breeze rustling some leaves here and there, and the stream gurgling as background.

The Hare's smile fades, and Sam isn't sure if she is relieved to see less of its teeth or not.

I want to make a vow. That's what she should say, like she told Pamela. *Help me make a vow.* That's not quite right either, but it's close. Closer.

Help me.

Sam opens her mouth to say that, or something, but instead she thinks of the man, John, in his scrappy clothes and with his tangled, wispy beard. He had asked her not to. Not to make a vow, that he wasn't ready, whatever that meant.

She closes her mouth, and the Hare stares at her for a moment more and then turns away. It does so uncertainly, and part way it pauses and looks back. Then its smile returns, wide and toothy, and it unlocks its fingers and makes a funny little twiddling wave with both hands – *bye bye.* Maybe it's *bye for now.* Maybe *bye forever, you had your chance.*

It takes a couple of slow, long, loping steps on its hind legs and then is gone between the trees where it should have no cover, where it should be easily still visible.

But it's gone anyway.

The sound of the stream is louder, busy and cheerful and uncaring, but Sam hasn't come upon it yet. The path is loose white gravel, almost as if it has been carefully strewn and maintained like it is over time. The small stones roll underfoot, and more than once she has almost gone over.

She's looking for the Hare. She's looking for John. Looking, looking. She has chosen at random each time the path has forked, and she should have come to something by now instead of trees and grass and rocks. The path, each path, is all tiny pebbles and uncertainty.

It feels like work. More, it feels like life.

She reaches yet another fork, one path narrow, one wider but twisting, curving behind one large tree and then going up and over a small rumple in the valley floor. She takes this one, shying away from the narrow, and tries to ignore the way the flat blue sky presses down like a ceiling. The Valley is bigger than it is, and also not. It is a box like the stationery cupboard, but not. This box is full of unknowns and decisions and ways that are slippery underfoot.

"Why are you asking about the Valley?" the barista at Perky Grind asks. She is short and has spiky hair and is extremely, aggressively efficient with both her drink-making and her words. She is espresso in human form—*bam, bam, bam.* Words, actions. Glare. Her name is Pamela, it says so on her pink tag. Sam comes in here every day, and has never noticed

Pamela's name tag before. She has also never noticed the Hare tattoo on her wrist.

Sam has ordered a dirty chai like usual, and Pamela is quick in whipping it up. Shot, milk, steam, chai powder. Pamela isn't angry, no. Just... sure. Violently sure, and quick. Too quick, and here she is, holding the drink out and waiting for Sam to answer her rebuttal question, not mucking about, making sure the whole of what Sam has asked, what she is thinking of is real and out in the world.

"I work with a guy called Jerry," Sam says, which isn't an answer.

Pamela snorts. "He didn't even mean to go there," she says. "He got lost on a walk, so he says."

"You meant to, though," Sam says. Pamela says nothing, but half rolls her eyes. *Sure. Duh.*

"I want to make a vow," Sam goes on, stumbling over the words even though they are the obvious next thing to say.

Pamela puts the drink down on the counter and gives Sam a pretty severe look, for a barista.

"You don't seem like the type," she says.

"What do I seem like, then?" Sam asks. Now that's a good question, and one she would like someone to answer, but Pamela doesn't say anything to that.

"You made a vow," Sam adds.

Pamela nods but doesn't offer anything in the way of vow-explanation. Jerry didn't offer any of his vow details either, even when she had asked. He had just smiled his too-thin smile.

Vows don't get bandied about.

The person waiting to order waves like that will make them more visible. Pamela holds up a finger at them.

"You know the way to start. Everyone does. Just catch the bus to the start of the trail. I don't even know why Jerry sent you to me," Pamela says. The words are a dismissal, but she doesn't turn to her next customer.

"I..." the words don't come easily. That's no surprise. They hadn't come at all in the stationery (stationary) closet with Jerry either, he of the soft smile and thin hair.

"Are you happy?" she asks.

Pamela takes a half-step back and her eyes widen like she has been slapped or something. Then she shakes her head and turns away, back to her bam bam bam coffee-making.

"It's not about happiness," she says over her shoulder. "It's about what you want."

Sam doesn't like that answer. All she knows is she doesn't want to be stationary, she doesn't want to be in that box of her life.

But she also wants to be.

If the Valley is a box, then John really should be called Jack. He pops out from behind a tree next to the path, his grey beard sad, gappy and unkempt, his eyes wild. There is a Hare tattoo on his neck, half-obscured by a smear of dirt.

"Are you free?" he whispers, and she stares at him, uncomprehending.

"I mean, did you feel it? Did you make a vow?" he adds as he comes out from behind the tree and stands on the path in his old leather shoes. He is holding a long stick.

"What did you mean, bait?" Sam asks.

John grins in a less than reassuring way and holds up his stick. The end is kind of sharp, like it's been rubbed down on a rock or flat surface. He pokes the air with it.

"Yah! Yah!" he says, excited. "I'm going to kill that fucking rabbit!"

"What?" Sam blurts, too surprised to be alarmed at this outburst, this child-like enthusiasm.

He comes close, too close for comfort, and Sam can smell his earthy scent, almost rank.

"Did you feel it?" he asks. "Did you cave?"

"Feel what?" Sam asks. She wants to step back from him but also doesn't want to, because that might be dangerous.

"Good," he says. "That thing will push for you to make your vow, and then you'll be stuck."

He waves the stick again, poking at the air, and this time he makes little grunting noises to go with the motion.

"Are... are you stuck?" Sam asks, not quite sure what she means. She has no idea what he is even doing in the Valley, if the Valley decides who gets in. It let her in though, so maybe it is clueless.

John's gaze snaps back to her and she does take a step back.

"You just hold out," he says. "And when the thing is distracted—" he pokes with the stick again. "Yah! Then I'll get my life back."

Sam doesn't know what to say to that. The Hare did not push her to make any vow. Maybe it ran away too quickly or something.

Maybe she's defective.

Speaking of running away, John darts off the path and behind a tree. She sees him flit between a couple more, not quite stealthy but not very loud. He isn't like the Hare, just eerily disappearing, but after watching him go for a moment, she stops looking.

John might have his own box to try and get out of.

It's later, which is about all Sam can tell. She turns a corner on the twisty path where it slips between two tall grey rocks and the flatness of the air is suddenly right *there*, right in front of her. She can tell, even though it looks the same because it is just too flat, a wall, the edge of a box. It's easy to see a thing when you love it and hate it so.

Sam puts a hand out, slowly. The air just in front of her is flat, firm but not strong, and after a moment of hesitation, she pushes on it. It is either that or go back, pick another path, and she is pretty sure another path isn't going to get her anywhere different.

The air gives. She stumbles forward to find herself in the early evening.

It's not the Valley, not even a bit. She is standing on a street surrounded by long shadows. In front of her it's not picturesque suburbia or anything. There is a lot of traffic on the street and parking looks to be troublesome. There is a house in front of her which is really a narrow-shouldered townhouse sandwiched in a row of them, one of many soldiers facing the small city centre that is visible beyond similar rows of buildings. It's her city, her glorified town, for whatever that is worth. She knows that greyness, that smell of sad urban trees bound by concrete, the air that tastes of car oil and hurry, the hymn of traffic on the bypass. Those things are the dull walls of her days.

Jerry stands on the sidewalk next to Sam, just below the steps to the narrow dwelling. The lights are on inside, and even though the townhouse is small and looks kind of squeezed, there is something of depth to it. Maybe it isn't the building—maybe it's just that smile on Jerry's face, the same one he shows everyone at work. He is looking up at those windows and he is just himself. No more, no less.

"Are you happy?" she asks, like she did in the stationery cupboard.

He doesn't seem to hear her. Doesn't even acknowledge her. He just puts one foot on the first step and starts up towards the door and she figures either she isn't there or he isn't real, or whatever he would say is his vow and thus not up for discussion.

But then he does speak, softly. He doesn't look away from the house, from those lighted windows, and his smile doesn't shift.

"I'm working on it," he says.

That's it for the street. It turns into the sunlight of the Valley before Jerry takes another step and Sam is standing on the path, staring at all that white gravel that so does not approve of her feet upon it.

She starts walking again, because it's either that or, well... that. She doesn't know how long she is on the path this time, but it forks again and again and she goes left or right with no regard. The blue sky is flat above her and even though the world of the Valley should be small enough she has not even reached the stream. On and on, and it is like she is at work, in the dimness in front of the post-it notes. It is like she is on pause.

Finally she takes one fork onto a narrow path that slopes down, and she sees the stream below her. It is small and clear and gurgling as if in conversation with itself. It makes her thirsty, but only a little.

The path is very narrow but there is low grass verging it, and as she walks she realizes the Hare is next to her. It is doing its weird waddling thing on its back legs, its long fingers folded together on its chest instead of placing them on the ground like a real Hare would do. It is only looking forward, its baby-pink face bland.

"There's a guy who wants to kill you with a stick," Sam says, because it seems like that's a decent thing to do. The Hare waddles on, but she sees it roll its eyes towards her for a moment.

"Unsatisfied customer?" she asks. The Hare does not respond. Maybe it can't. Maybe the Hare of the Valley of Unbreakable Vows cannot speak.

They walk on for a bit. The stream is getting close, and then all of a sudden they are on the edge of it, where the path turns and runs along, up and down and over worn stones and muddy little rivulets.

Sam stops, and the Hare does too. It turns to Sam and smiles with its perfect teeth. It is very large, and it is looking down at her slightly.

"How does this work, then?" Sam asks. "John says you will push me to make a vow. That I will feel it."

The Hare says nothing, just smiles. She feels nothing. She feels like she is still on pause.

"Come on then!" she snaps.

The Hare smiles a bit more. Then, frighteningly quickly, it unlaces its long-fingered hands each from the other and shoves Sam hard in the chest.

Sam falls into the water which is cold and very shallow and in the second before her butt hits the rocky bottom she is not there at all.

She isn't on a suburban street either, and the softly smiling Jerry is absent.

There are bright lights and music that is too loud mostly because the room she is in is too small for the thumping beat. Sam winces and sits up, shading her eyes.

Someone is crying. It isn't soft, and it isn't raging, but it is worn and hiccup-y, the sound of someone who is tired of how they feel. As her eyes adjust Sam sees a bench with several large sheets of paper, some with outlines, a few with swirls of pastel colours, mostly pale sky blues, bright but abject, all of them abandoned, half-done things that are beautiful. The crying is coming from behind an easel. Sam stands slowly and shuffles around until she can see the girl sitting on the low stool facing whatever she is working on, or has stopped working on.

It's Pamela of the spiky hair and impatience. She holds a fat blue marker of some artsy type, and there are mostly dried tracks of tears down her cheeks. She is glaring at whatever is on the easel, and Sam almost moves so she can see. Almost, but no.

“Are you okay?” she asks, in case this is real. Jerry had maybe been real, had maybe heard her.

Had maybe answered.

Pamela grimaces and then leans forward, slashing at the paper or canvas or whatever is on the easel with the fat marker. Not angry, not quite, but with that same frantic hurry, the economy of steaming milk, packed coffee grinds, orders served.

But there is no order to be filled here. No dirty chai pushed across the bench, no next customer. Pamela scowls and a tear runs and she breathes hard as she drops the marker and then snatches up a thick brush that has been resting in a small tin. It drips with dark paint as she starts in, and now Sam does not want to look at the easel. It seems a private thing, a violently frantic private thing.

Pamela smiles and sobs and laughs.

“Pamela?” Sam asks. “Is this your vow?”

“Something has to work. Something has to change,” Pamela says, smiling and crying. Like with Jerry, Sam is not sure if the words are for her, or if they are even real.

Then the floor is gone and she is falling backwards and there is a nasty, sharp pain in her butt and her pants are wet.

John is standing over her, his bare feet in the water but only to his ankles because the stream is barely more than a wide trickle. His stick is raised.

“Yah!” he says, and thrusts the stick towards the Hare, which is sitting back on its haunches on the edge of the stream. It is far enough away that the stick is not even close, and frankly, John is ridiculous. His stick is a thin and sad thing and he is wild and grimy and old and should take advantage of the stream more often.

But he is also weird and violent and Sam stays sitting in the water with at least two sharp stones digging into her left butt cheek.

The Hare doesn't move. It is smiling again, or still smiling, and as John thrusts a second time it rolls its eyes in the most human way ever and smiles even wider. Then it raises its hands up near its head, its long pink fingers pointing up. *Oh no. I surrender.*

John, emboldened, takes a step towards it and Sam struggles to her own feet.

"Stop!" she yells. She isn't on pause anymore. She has no fucking idea about vows or what she has seen or what John has done or had done to him, but she doesn't want to see what might happen next. She grabs his arm.

"Stop!" she says again, and he turns to her, his eyes bug-wild and wide.

"I've made no vow!" she yells right into his face, with no idea why this might matter. "I don't even have something I want!"

John isn't listening. The Hare has surrendered and he has his moment. He leaps forward, thrusting with his puny stick, and the Hare smiles and rolls its eyes, this time towards Sam. *Can you believe this guy?*

Then the stick with its badly sharpened point goes straight into the Hare's throat and those fine-fingered hands come down and grasp the stick, not in shock or horror but like they are caressing it, taking it in, holding it. Accepting it.

The Hare falls to the side, silent and still smiling, its eyes on Sam, its hands wrapped around the stick, and John is laughing and Sam is screaming and then John is crying, kneeling on the bank in the mud.

It is late afternoon, finally, the sun painting the trees orange and pink and the sky deepening with the same colours. More, the sky is opening up.

John has eaten the last of Sam's muesli bars.

"Did it work?" she asks him as they sit on a rock a little up the path from the dead Hare. The creature doesn't look any smaller now that it is dead. It is brown and grey and too still, and she is glad she can't see its face from where they sit.

I'm working on it.

Something has to work.

Something has to change.

He sucks on his teeth. He won't look at the Hare, hasn't since she led him to the rock and sat him down.

"I don't... no," he says, very low. "No, it didn't work."

She doesn't ask how he knows. She came all this way and made no vow herself. She has no idea why the Valley even let her in, or why the Hare did.

"Did you know when you first saw the Hare?" she asks. "What your vow would be?"

He stares at her for what seems a long time, then his gaze finally does turn to the dead Hare. There is a light breeze, and its fur ruffles slightly. Those elegant fingers are just visible on the stick, wrapped loosely, lovingly. If this were some story John would become the Hare, or the Hare would disappear, or the Valley would crumble, pieces of the sky falling in like the thin walls they are.

None of those things happen.

"I... I brought my vow with me," John says. "Inside."

He draws a deep breath, looks away from the Hare, then back. "Maybe it's not the Hare that makes it Unbreakable. Maybe its not the Valley. Maybe..."

He shakes his head, and when he speaks next his voice is low and cracked and he is so very old, so much older than he was already.

"Oh no," he says.

Sam is enjoying the dimness when the door opens behind her. She thinks it is going to be Jerry, must be him with his smile and his certainty and his *working on it*.

And it is, of course, because sometimes these things just happen how they are going to happen.

"Hiding?" he asks, his voice kind, his head cocked slightly to one side. He wants to ask, she can tell. He wants to know. She can see him scanning her arms, her neck, her exposed skin for a tattoo that isn't there.

Sam thinks of John. *Yah! Yah!* A child with a stick, staying in the Valley for who-knows how long, hiding, creeping, looking everywhere but inside, wanting only to stab at a trap of his own making. The way the Hare smiled as if it knew exactly what was coming—*oh no. I surrender*. How it had held the stick in the end, like it had expected it. How nothing had changed when it lay still on the ground, its fur moving only with the breeze.

She hears John again. *Oh no.*

She thinks of Pamela, her furious efficiency, the ache in her voice as she holds her dripping brush. *Something has to change. Something has to work.* Crying and laughing and coming at her easel like it is a series of tasks she has set for herself, like there is an end like a dirty chai, a cup for a customer if only she can get the order right, the process in place, as the beat of music bounces off the walls and fills the air of the small room.

And Jerry. *I'm working on it,* as he walks up to the townhouse that is so deep, so squeezed, so narrow. His soft smile, which is either acceptance or surrender or both.

"I'm just taking a pause," Sam says, and the word tastes like relief, finally, and the stationery cupboard is nothing but a cupboard.

"But I'm not going to stay in this box any more."

The Person You See

I stitch my hope together early,
Binding my flaws under the pink sunrise.
With your love at my back
I venture out, the person you see
somewhere before me.

I seek your eyes in every face,
Searching for the person you see, reflected
even as my threads loosen.
And when I fall short and fall down,
When I fall apart
and the shadows grow long
I bring the pieces of myself and
the pieces of my hope back to you.

And you smile
Because you know I am eager for the dawn,
and to try again
for the person you see.

Acknowledgements

Always, always, Kara and the kids come first. Kara, I want to be the person you see. Kevin, Casey, Maeve, I am trying to be the best Dad I can. I want all the happiness for you, and if there is true emotion in any of these stories, it is because you have taught me love and fear of loss, as well as joy — so much of all three.

Thanks to Pamela and Samantha, who make me laugh, and the Horror Critters Louise, Pauline, Tracie and Julie, who are such a touchstone. My people! I found you! Double thanks to Pamela for her beautiful cover, which I have spent far too long just staring at, and to Noel for his deft editing hand. I must also mention with gratitude Maddison Stoff, who swept in with deft and insightful sensitivity reading as well as kind words and encouragement.

Some of the stories in this collection have been published elsewhere. For those, I wish to thank those first readers and editors who saw something in the tales, and gave them the chance to be read by others. I appreciate you and the work you put into keeping short fiction alive and vibrant.

I also want to thank anyone who has read any of these stories. Thank you for your time—it is valuable, and I feel honoured that you would give some of it to what I have written. I hope you feel it was time well spent.

Publication History

"Market of Loss" First published in *Aurealis* Issue 176, November 2024. (Winner, Best Fantasy Short Story, Aurealis Awards. Finalist, Best Short Story, Ditmar Awards).

"You Don't Get to Choose Entanglement" First published in *Nature: Futures*, 11th August 2021.

"Ben Builds Boats" Original to this collection.

"Heart of the Gestalt" First published in *Nature: Futures*, 10th March 2021.

"A Future in Ashes" First published in *Haven Speculative*, Issue 15 2024.

"Three Possible Muses" First published in *Nature Futures*, 10th April 2024.

"Skins" Original to this collection.

"The Botanical Garden of Purgation" Original to this collection.

"You, Spinning" Original to this collection.

"Change YourView" First published in *Nature: Futures*, 26th April 2023. (Finalist, Best Science Fiction Short Story, Aurealis Awards).

"As Brittle as Granite" First published in *Cast of Wonders* Episode 646, 2025.

"Fermi's Paradox Box" Original to this collection.

"Maintenance" First published in *Nature: Futures*, 12th September 2025.

"The Complete and Utter Drag of Becoming the Self-Taught Ghost Poet of Mars" First published in *the Conflux 19 Brave New Worlds! programme*. (Second place, Conflux 19 short story competition).

"Location, Velocity, End Point" First published in *Nature: Futures*, 7th December 2022.

"Universes all the way Down" First published in *Nature: Futures*, 9th September 2020.

"Optimal Care" First published in *Cast of Wonders* Episode 615, 2024.

"The Scythe and the Grey Witch" Original to this collection.

"Farming with Cranky" First published in *Little Blue Marble*, 23rd December 2022.

"Prometheus, Burning" Original to this collection.

“Diamonds are Forever” Original to this collection.

“Goldbergian Physics” First published in *Nature: Futures*, 10th November 2021.

“The Plumber” First published in *Gotta Wear Eclipse Glasses*, Third Flatiron Publishing, 2020.

“Love and Thorns” Original to this collection.

“Better World” First published in *Factor Four* Issue 43, 2025.

“Unfurl” Original to this collection.

“The Skin Trader” First published in *Daily Science Fiction*, 28th February, 2022.

“Blipcoin” First published in *Nature: Futures*, 10th August 2022.

“The Downloaded Detective and the Swollen Technician” Original to this collection.

“Stutter” Original to this collection.

"Samantha's Encounter with the Giant Hare in the Valley of Unbreakable Vows, and what came of It" Original to this collection.

“The Person You See” Original to this collection.

Also By the Author

Drowning in the Dark and Other Stories, IFWG Publishing International.

About the Author

Matt Tighe is a father, husband, writer, and environmental scientist. He lives on a small farm in northeastern New South Wales Australia with his patient wife, amazing children, and far too many animals. He has won some writing awards and competitions. He is also a Professor in his day job, teaching and researching pollution management, conservation, and applied statistics. You can find him on bluesky @mktighewrites.bsky.social or online at matttighe.weebly.com.

www.ingramcontent.com/pod-product-compliance
Lightning Source LLC
LaVergne TN
LVHW050621100826
845148LV00011B/1679

* 9 7 8 0 6 4 8 1 4 4 2 9 8 *